A

HUMMINGBIRD'S

NEST

a hummingbird's nest

A NOVEL

RUSSO SHANIDZE

BASED ON TRUE EVENTS

Palmetto Publishing Group
Charleston, SC

A Hummingbird's Nest
Copyright © 2019 by Russo Shanidze

All rights reserved. This book or any portion thereof may not be reproduced or used in any manner whatsoever without the express written permission of the publisher except for the use of brief quotations in a book review.

First Edition

Printed in the United States

Hardcover: 9781641114639
Paperback: 9781641114493
Ebook: 9781641114646

Prologue

Growing up under oppression in the Eastern Bloc, Sofia could only dream of living in a country where she was free to express her artistic talents and creativity using the international education that she had achieved. After the borders opened, she turned her dream into reality and moved to California with her one-year-old son, unaware of how difficult life would be for a single mom in a brand-new city with no family support around her. But she persevered and finally built a comfortable life and home in the City of Angels. Then most unexpectedly, she met a man who seemed to be her perfect match. Their romance was intense, passionate, fun, and spontaneous. He was wealthy, genuine, and loyal; treated her like a princess; and seemed honest to a fault. Then one day the walls came tumbling down, and Sofia's world was crushed. But in her typical style, she pulled herself up and turned adversity into opportunity. Follow Sofia on her journey of resilience and redemption as she negotiates the challenges of life in *A Hummingbird's Nest*.

Los Angeles, California – 2017

Sofia Novak was a single mom in her late thirties. She had raised her son, Nick, without any support from his father because he had died when Nick was just one year old. Sofia dedicated her life mostly to Nick and never thought of having any serious relationships. But when Nick turned thirteen, Sofia thought that he was old enough to be a little independent, and she decided to socialize on a limited basis. Sofia had immigrated to the United States from Poland twelve years ago, and she had a slight accent. She was five feet five and thin with short curly blond hair and porcelain skin. Sofia was a well-educated, smart, independent, humble, sweet, and elegant woman. Her hobbies were playing piano and writing poems. She also was a great Polish folk dancer. Over the years she had worked extremely hard to create a stable income to support herself and her son.

Recently Sofia and her friend Katarina had started their own web series. They both had worked tirelessly to make their dreams come true.

Katarina was in her early to mid-thirties and was married with two boys, aged twelve and fourteen. She and her husband were originally from Lebanon. Katarina was thin, tall, between five feet nine and five feet ten, and a brunette with long curly hair. She had big green eyes and was an attractive young woman. She was feminine, smart, generous, kind, very sweet, and sensitive, and at the same time, she could be tough and strong. She and Sofia were very close and loved each other as only dear friends could. Katarina was always very supportive of Sofia and was always there for her.

SOFIA'S APARTMENT—DAY

It was a very exciting day in Sofia's apartment. Sofia and Katarina had just finished their first day of shooting for their web series, and they sat down in the living room to rest. The casting crew moved things around and cleaned up the whole apartment. After a few minutes, Katarina got up, grabbed her bag, and was ready to leave. She looked at Sofia and said in her sweet voice, "We have to go out tonight and celebrate our first shooting day."

Sofia looked very tired, and her voice was fragile. "No, I can't Kat! I think I'm getting sick. I'm not feeling well, and I've got so much to do at home."

Katarina responded, "Get ready. I'm taking you, and we're going out tonight. You never have time for yourself. You can't just work all the time. You need to have some fun. We have to celebrate the start of our new project. I'll pick you up at 7:00 p.m."

ROYAL RUAL HOTEL, RESTAURANT—EVENING

Katarina and Sofia were having dinner in the restaurant, and they both looked very joyful and talkative. Even though Sofia had a sore throat and asked the waitress for a cup of tea with honey and lemon, she still seemed very happy and content.

"It's so great to feel free for just a couple of hours—no kids, no husband, just us, Sofia."

"I agree…" Sofia sighed. "You can't even imagine how grateful I am right now. Thanks for making me come here tonight. Although I was not feeling well at home, now I feel great! The music and atmosphere are so serene…It feels…so relaxing. Maybe we should take a selfie."

At the dinner table next to Katarina and Sofia, there were two men having dinner. One man was in his late seventies or early eighties, was wearing a very stylish hat, and looked very classy. The other one was in his early fifties with dark hair. He was fit, well dressed, and an attractive-looking man. The younger man offered to take a picture of the two of them.

"Would you like me to take photos of you ladies?" The younger man asked.

Sofia looked at him, and without missing a beat, she replied, "Sure."

She passed her phone to the younger man, and he took a few photos of her and Katarina. Then he asked if the men could join the ladies for the night. Katarina and Sofia were reluctant to say anything. They glanced at each other, and finally, Sofia spoke up: "Yes, of course." She smiled but wasn't very certain about her decision.

The two men joined Sofia and Katarina at their dinner table. They introduced themselves and revealed that they were stepfather and son. The stepfather, Carlos, sat next to Katarina, and the son, Marco, sat very close to Sofia on the sofa. Sofia felt a little uncomfortable, and she moved herself away from Marco a little bit.

Marco instantly became very curious about Sofia. "Where are you originally from?" Marco asked.

"From Poland," Sofia replied.

"Wow...I don't really remember if I ever met anyone from Poland. How long have you been in the US, and what do you do?"

"I've been here for twelve years. I'm a single mom and have a thirteen-year-old son. Right now I'm working with my friend Katarina, and we're producing a web series. Today we shot our first episode and decided to celebrate our new venture, so we came here." Sofia was not interested in him at all, so she didn't ask any questions about him.

Marco just started talking about himself briefly; he lived in Beverly Hills, and his office was close to the hotel. Sofia was not really paying attention to what he was saying but just listened to him. There was a singer with a live band, and they were playing Latin American music. Carlos, Marco's stepfather, asked Sofia to dance. Sofia got up and joined Carlos on the dance floor. Carlos was an amazing dancer and so was Sofia. Marco could not take his eyes off Sofia while she danced with Carlos. He said to Katarina, "Sofia is amazing! She is quite elegant and classy and dances beautifully. You can tell that she's a real dancer. Please, please, tell her that I'd really like to see her again."

Katarina was quiet and did not say anything at first. Then she smiled and said, "Actually, Sofia is a professional folk dancer—that's why she's so good. But I can't dance."

Marco kept staring at Sofia. Katarina noticed it and knew that Marco was really into her. After Sofia and Carlos's dance finished, Carlos started dancing with Katarina. Sofia went back and sat next to Marco. Marco was leaning toward her and wanted to hug her, but Sofia pushed him back and said, "No hugging."

Marco apologized and tried to put honey into her tea. "Sofia, I would love to see you again sometime. Would that be possible?"

"I don't know, maybe." Sofia was very uncertain and still wasn't feeling well. Marco politely asked Sofia for her cell phone number. He got his phone out and impatiently waited to type her number. Sofia liked Marco's stepfather very much, so she felt OK about giving Marco her contact information. She took his phone from his hand and typed her number. After their dance, Carlos and Katarina came back to the table and everyone said goodbye to one another. The two men gave warm hugs to Katarina and Sofia, and they left.

"Oh my God, Sofia, that man is crazy about you! He couldn't stop talking about you, and he is so interested in seeing you again. If he calls you, please, please, give him a chance. He seems like a good, decent man." Sofia was quiet while listening to Katarina and didn't say a word. She just kept drinking her tea with honey and lemon.

One Month Later

Katarina and Sofia were shooting an episode of their web series in Sofia's apartment when Sofia received a text from Marco. This surprised her.

"Hi, Sofia, I hope you and your son are doing well. Are you free for lunch or dinner this week?"

"Hi, Marco, nice to hear from you! I hope all is well with you and your father. I'd be happy to meet you for lunch or dinner, but this week I'm very busy. How about next week?"

"That sounds perfect. I'll contact you next week. Have a great week."

One Week Later

THE LITTLE LIGHT RESTAURANT—EVENING

Marco and Sofia were sitting at the dinner table and were enjoying their night. This was their first date.

"My father has been very sick this past week, and we've been going back and forth to the emergency room. It's been really crazy. But while I was in the hospital watching my dad so sick and weak, I was thinking about the last time that he danced. I recalled that day when I met you and your friend at the Royal Rual Hotel, and the last time that he danced was there with you. Thinking about that made me want to see you, so I texted you right away from the hospital. I was lucky that you were willing to see me."

"Oh, Marco, so many things have happened since we met. I'm so sorry about your dad. He's such a high-spirited man. I love his energy, and he's a fabulous dancer. My thoughts and prayers are with him right now. But Marco, tell me about you."

"Well, right now I want you to know that I'm happy that I'm here with you!" Marco told Sofia briefly about his past and his past relationships. "I was married once for eight years. I was thirty-one when I met my wife, and I proposed to her in six weeks. I fell in love with her so quickly, and we got married six months later. The only problem we had was that she wanted to have kids and I didn't. Because of that, eight years later, we decided to divorce. After that I had two fiancés, but I never went through with either marriage for the same reason. I hated kids and never wanted them probably because I had a lousy childhood. But now I'm fine with kids, and I even regret that I don't have one. I know you have a son, and I'm glad that you do."

Marco continued telling Sofia his childhood story. "My father left us when I was six months old. He was originally from Italy. My mom was very young and raised me by herself. But she was very mean and harsh on me, always screaming, yelling, and throwing things at me. Sometimes she'd say, 'I want to kill you,' and as a little boy, I repeated the same things, throwing things back at her and yelling at her and saying, 'I want to kill you too.' I was six when my mom met my stepdad; he was originally from Colombia, and they got married when I was eight. Carlos had a horrible temper then, and he was always yelling and screaming at my mom. They used to fight every single day. I hated being with them, especially going out with them together, because they fought all the time. Even though I had a younger sister, I couldn't wait to grow up and leave my parents' house. So basically, my childhood was miserable, and I never had any peace or love.

"But when I was eighteen, I left my house and never went back. I took care of myself, started working and building my own life. I never ever got any financial help from my family but I became independent at a very young age. Sales and marketing really interested me, so I took that direction. Finally, years and years later, I started my own real estate business, worked extremely hard, and created a secure life for myself. And that's where I am now. I also consider myself very lucky. Additionally, years later in my adulthood, I became closer to my stepdad, and now we have a more peaceful relationship. But I think I talked too much, and now I want to hear your story. Sofia, please tell me about you."

Sofia was listening to Marco attentively. "Wow, it's so hard to hear about your childhood. I feel bad when I hear stories like that because I'm a mom, too, and I've been raising my son by myself for all of these years. I never got any help from his dad because he died when my son was just one year old. Now he's thirteen, and he's a very good boy. I had actually divorced his dad before he died because he was an alcoholic. He tried to quit but, unfortunately, couldn't do it. I helped him as much as I could, but I finally realized that I was powerless. No one can help you unless you help yourself, right? So I gave up. I wanted my son to have a healthy life, and I didn't want him to watch his father's pain, addiction, and struggle.

"So my son and I immigrated to the United States from Poland twelve years ago, and we're both very lucky to be here. I have been in the media industry for so many years, and while working, I've been constantly trying to expand my skills in different fields, such as acting, voice-over, writing, and producing. Regarding my family, unlike you, I had a wonderful childhood. My parents are extraordinary people, and they were always there for me and are still very supportive of me. My mom is a musician; she plays piano beautifully and taught piano for many years. My dad was a small business owner, which was very difficult in Poland. But they both worked very hard, and now they're retired. Currently they live in Boston, close to my older brother. I love them all, and I'm blessed that I have them in my life. Can I ask you a question? What did you like about me that night that you decided to join us at the hotel?"

"Your vibrant energy—it was so contagious. I could tell that you're a very strong, independent, and at the same time, classy and elegant woman. I really, really wanted to see you again."

"Really? Thanks for the compliment." Sofia took a drink of her champagne and smiled. "Honestly, I wouldn't have seen you again if not for my friend Katarina. She's the one who told me that you were interested in me and that you seemed like a very nice man. She was saying, 'Please, please, give him a chance and just go out with him once.' But what I didn't like about you was that you were trying to touch me all the time and wanted to hug me. I don't like that, especially from a stranger that I just met. I didn't know you at all." They both started to laugh. "That was annoying, and on top of that, I wasn't feeling well. But your father is an amazing dancer—I loved his style."

"Wow…then I truly owe Katarina. I have to thank her. I'm so glad that we met again." After the dinner they both got up and left the restaurant. Marco opened the car door for Sofia and drove her back home. When they reached Sofia's home, they said goodbye to each other with a hug only, and Sofia walked up the stairs into her apartment. Marco went back to his car and left.

SOFIA'S APARTMENT—EVENING

Sofia was in her kitchen preparing dinner, and her son, Nick, was setting the table. Nick was tall, thin with dark blond hair, and had light skin. He was always helpful to his mom.

"Nick, I want to tell you something. I started dating a very nice man. His name is Marco, and I really like him. He treats me very respectfully and is an intelligent and kind man."

Nick's eyes were getting big. He was thrilled to hear that his mom was finally, after all these years, going out with someone. "Mom, I'm so, so happy for you. I've been waiting for this for a long time!" Suddenly, Nick ran to his room and was looking for something that he kept in his secret place. He found the little piece of paper and brought it back to his mom.

"Mom, read this…this is my Christmas wish list." Sofia looked at the list and read it out loud: "Xbox, two NBA Xbox games, two movies, I want my mom to have a boyfriend, I want a stepdad." Sofia could not believe it. "Oh my God, honey, this is what you wanted for Christmas?" They both looked at each other and smiled, and Sofia gave her son a warm hug.

Later that evening Sofia had just come out of the bathroom and was heading to bed. She picked up her favorite book of poems, got into bed, and as soon as she started reading, Marco called.

"Hi, Sofia, how are you?"

"I'm good. I just got into bed and am reading… poems."

"I love poetry too. I used to write poems when I was a child, and I still write them now and then when I'm in a poetry mood. Listen, are you available on Friday at 7:30 p.m.? We can go out dancing."

"Oh, I would love to go dancing with you. I hope your father is doing better. How is he?"

"He's doing much better and is back home. I pray that everything will be fine with him. I've started writing a poem about him and wanted to share it with you. I'll text it to you now."

Sofia received the following poem from Marco:

I feel the loneliness approaching and think of all
my mistakes.
My life and his absence will only make them
more obvious.
Untethered for the first time and afraid,
My best friend will no longer be.
I am not unique and know this moment shall pass,
but the memory will remain.

"That is very beautiful and touching, but there's so much pain and sorrow in those words. I see how bonded you and your father are. Please keep writing—I want to hear more of your poems. I love poetry and I write it, too, when I get the inspiration."

"See you on Friday, Sofia. Have a good night."

"Good night, Marco"

ROYAL RUAL HOTEL, RESTAURANT—EVENING

There was a live orchestra playing with a singer in the restaurant. On the dance floor, Sofia and Marco were dancing and enjoying the night. They stayed on the floor through a couple of songs. After the dances they sat down at their table.

"You dance beautifully. Is there anything you can't do?" Marco said.

"Oh, thank you…but…" Sofia sighed. "There are a lot of things I can't do. I'm terrible at math, and my son always complains about it because I can't help him." They both started laughing.

"How's Nick doing? And what does he like? Any sports?"

"He's doing very well at school. I can't complain. I'm very lucky that he's a good teenager. He loves basketball, and his favorite team is the Cleveland Cavaliers because LeBron James is his favorite player. He makes me watch all of his games. But I support the Golden State Warriors, and I love Stephen Curry, so Nick and I have a little rivalry there!"

"Oh really? I love LeBron too. I'm on Nick's side! So I'll check out the games and get tickets for all of us." Marco was so excited that he got out his phone and started checking the game schedule. The music continued. Soon after, Marco and Sofia walked to the car outside. Marco opened the car door for Sofia and took her back home in his Ferrari. While they were driving, Marco said to Sofia, "I know that you know lots of poems. Would you recite some for me please? I really want to hear them."

Sofia was so passionate about poems that she just started reciting them nonstop in different languages. She started in English first.

> *Even after all this time*
> *The sun never says to the earth,*
> *"You owe me."*
> *Look what happens with a love like that,*
> *It lights the whole sky.*
> *—Hafiz*

The earth lifts its glass to the sun
And light—light is poured.
I lift my heart to God
And grace is poured...
—Hafiz

"Hope" is the thing with feathers –
That perches in the soul –
And sings the tune without the words –
And never stops – at all...
—Emily Dickinson

When you see me sitting quietly,
Like a sack left on the shelf,
Don't think I need your chattering.
I'm listening to myself...
—Maya Angelou

"You are amazing!" Marco said.

Then Sofia continued in French. Marco was very impressed as he witnessed Sofia's command and love of poetry.

They arrived at Sofia's apartment and after parking in front of it, Marco opened the car door for her and helped her out of the car. He asked Sofia for a kiss, but Sofia didn't oblige him.

"Just a kiss?"

Sofia replied, "This is not just a kiss, Marco. This is our first kiss, and I want it to be magical and memorable." She didn't kiss him but gave him a hug. "Thank you so much for a beautiful evening. Good night."

"OK, I'll think about how to make it magical. I had a wonderful evening with you too. Good night, Sofia." Marco repeated over and over to himself while walking back to his car, "A magical kiss, a magical kiss."

BASKETBALL COURT—DAY

Sofia was watching her son playing basketball with other kids, and she was excited because his team was winning. She received a text from Marco.

> "Dear Sofia,
> The playoffs started today, but right now the only games scheduled in LA are the Clippers with other playoff teams. I'd like to take you and Nick to one of those games this week."

Sofia did not want to rush and introduce Nick to Marco so quickly. She had only seen him twice, and although she liked him very much, she was still very cautious.

"Hi, Marco, thank you so much for your offer. Nick would love to go to a game, but the only teams he really wants to see play are the Golden State Warriors or the Cleveland Cavs. But thanks again, and have a wonderful day."

"Noted—talk to you soon. You have a great day too."

Sofia returned to watching Nick and his team play basketball.

DANCE STUDIO—DAY

Sofia and Katarina were shooting an episode about dancing for the web series. Sofia was performing a Polish folk dance when she received a call. Katarina picked up the phone for Sofia, looked at it, and saw that it was Marco.

"Your Marco is calling you," Kat said with a smile.

Sofia took the phone. "Hello, Marco."

"Hi, Sofia. How are you?"

"I'm great. I'm actually shooting a dance scene right now with my team."

"Oh, sounds exciting. I won't take much of your time, but I was wondering if you'd like to have dinner with me tonight. We can meet each other at the Adams Club at seven thirty, and my driver can pick you up at seven from your place. Will that work for you?"

"Yes, that sounds great. I look forward to seeing you. Thanks for the driver."

"Great, see you tonight."

THE ADAMS CLUB, ROOFTOP RESTAURANT—EVENING

A special table with candles was reserved for Sofia and Marco. They were enjoying the evening together. Marco treated Sofia very elegantly. He adored her and was impressed by her background and the way she was raised. He admired her qualities and values. A waiter approached their table. Marco asked the waiter to bring two glasses of pinot noir. The waiter took the order, nodded, and walked away.

"This is a beautiful place, Marco."

"I'm glad that you like it, and I'm so happy to see you again. You look beautiful as always, Sofia."

"Thank you! You look great too!"

Sofia smiled, and they both stared at each other lovingly, just enjoying the quiet moment. The waiter returned with their drinks.

"I'm a very lucky man. I have to thank Katarina, for sure, for convincing you to meet me. You're a very sweet woman, Sofia. I know you and Nick moved to LA recently, and there must be a lot of places you haven't been to. Besides your work, being an artist, dancer, writer and, of course, a great mom, I'm sure you're always busy! Is there anything else you like to do?" Marco asked.

"I love nature, water, and the ballet and opera very much. I don't even remember when the last time was that I saw an opera. And my son really keeps me busy along with everything else," Sofia replied with a smile.

"Wow, I love all of them too. Actually, I really love opera. It's been years since I've been to the opera house here in LA. We should definitely go one day. Are you ready to get out of here? Let's go. I want to show you something."

Sofia and Marco got up, left the restaurant, and walked to the elevator.

Marco pushed the second-floor button in the elevator. He held Sofia's hand, and they smiled at each other. They got out of the elevator and headed to the club's library. Once inside, Sofia was fascinated by the elegance of the little library that held an incredible collection of books, journals, and newspapers. She checked a few books, and Marco stood close to her, quietly looking at her. Marco then took Sofia around the club and showed her different rooms. It was 10:30 p.m., already late, and no one was in any of the rooms. The last room they entered was dark with just a little light shimmering through a window in the corner where a grand piano was standing by itself. Marco knew that Sofia's mom was a musician and played piano, but he didn't know that Sofia played as well. She sat down and started playing *Moonlight Sonata* by Beethoven. Marco was impressed by Sofia's talent and humbleness and leaned toward the piano, listening to Sofia very intently. When she got up, Marco embraced her and wanted to kiss her, but Sofia pulled herself back and said, "Marco, I'm not ready yet."

Marco respected Sofia's decision and kissed her on her cheek. Then he said, "What could be more magical than this place with you?"

Sofia didn't respond, and they both stood in silence.

SOFIA'S APARTMENT, LIVING ROOM—DAY

Sofia was rehearsing a scene with her actor friend Maddie. Maddie was in her early forties and was half Korean and half Puerto Rican. She was an attractive and exotic-looking woman between five feet two and five feet four with long dark straight hair. She was very smart, loving, caring, determined, and hard working with a very strong personality. Maddie lived with her boyfriend and his daughter. She was a very close and dear friend of Sofia's, and they were always there for each other. They often rehearsed and practiced their acting scenes together.

Maddie was performing, but when Sofia heard her phone beep, she apologized to Maddie and grabbed her phone.

"Sorry, Maddie, I need to check my phone for a second."

"Sure."

Sofia had received a text from Marco.

"Dear Sofia, I'm thinking of you. I hear you playing piano, and it brings me happiness."

"I'm thinking of you too, Marco. You're a wonderful man."

"I have a surprise for you. This Saturday I'm taking you out, but I can't tell you where. I'll send you the details later. I look forward to seeing you on Saturday at seven. My driver will pick you up at six thirty from your place."

"I love surprises, Marco. I look forward to seeing you on Saturday."

"What's going on Sofia? Are you dating someone?" Maddie had a big smile on her face.

"Yes, I started dating a very nice man. His name is Marco." Once Sofia started talking about Marco, her face lit up. "I met him at the Royal Rual Hotel last month with his father when Katarina and I were celebrating the start of our new web series. He treats me very nicely, and he's a very proper, decent, and smart man. I really like him. He's taking me out on Saturday, and it's a surprise!"

"Oh, Sofia, I'm so happy for you! You deserve a wonderful man in your life. You've been working so hard and raising Nick…You never have time for yourself! Now Nick's a big boy and more independent, so it's time for you to start thinking about your future. This is fantastic!"

"Yes, I'm very happy! Nick's really excited about me dating. He even told me that this was one of his Christmas wishes. Can you believe that?" Sofia's whole face was smiling with happiness.

"Nick definitely needs a man in his life. It's so important, especially for boys at this age, to have a male role model. I'm so happy for both of you," Maddie said.

"Thanks, Maddie." Sofia checked her watch. "OK, let's keep rehearsing. We don't have much time left before the audition."

Maddie and Sofia continued their rehearsal.

LOS ANGELES OPERA HOUSE—EVENING

Sofia and Marco were watching a performance of *Tosca*. Marco noticed how consumed Sofia was, and he was so appreciative that she was with him. After the opera they walked around downtown LA.

"You know what? I don't believe it when people say it takes time to fall in love with a person. Some say that like after five or six months, you've had enough time, and by then you should be in love with your partner. But it doesn't work like that for me. Either I fall in love with a woman right in the beginning, or I never do."

Marco put his hands around Sofia's waist and kissed her on her cheek. They looked at each other with warm smiles, then crossed the street together, got in the car, and went back to the Adams Club. When they entered the club, Marco remembered that upstairs there was a wedding going on.

"Let's crash the wedding and have some cake. I want something sweet. What do you think?" Marco asked.

"Sounds fun. Let's do it. I really want chocolate cake," Sofia replied.

The wedding room was beautifully decorated with flowers everywhere. Marco noticed that all the men in the room were wearing tuxedos and the women were in evening gowns. They looked very formal, and he started to feel a little uncomfortable about his cake caper. He told Sofia, "I don't think it's a good idea to do this because everyone is formally dressed and they can see that we don't belong to the party. Maybe we should go and find cake somewhere else."

"I don't think that anyone will notice that, but if you want, we can leave and go somewhere else." Sofia really wanted to stay because she loved everything about this place. It was a very classy and sophisticated wedding, and the atmosphere was extraordinary. As they were leaving the room, a very nice young lady approached them holding a big plate of a variety of cakes. "You guys are a very attractive-looking couple! Would you like some cake tonight?" She gave them a warm smile. Sofia and Marco were stunned, and they looked at each other before chuckling. They were so surprised that this woman had appeared out of nowhere. Both of them said "yes" and "thank you" at the same time without hesitation and with big smiles. Sofia took a piece of chocolate cake, and Marco tried the carrot cake. Marco took a few bites from Sofia's plate and said, "Sofia, you know what I really want?"

Sofia knew exactly what Marco wanted, but she was still reluctant and felt that the time hadn't come yet. Marco grabbed her hand after they were done with the cake and walked with her to the elevator. "Come with me. I want to show you something."

They both walked together down the hallway and were heading to the rooftop of the clubhouse.

There was a gorgeous view of the city from the rooftop where Sofia and Marco were standing together. They were on the top floor, and no one was there but them. The moon was shining, and the lights of the city made the evening sparkle.

"What do you think? Do you like it here?"

"This is magical, and..." Suddenly, Sofia saw a shooting star in the sky, and she knew that this was the moment. "There was a shooting star...Marco...I saw it..."

They finally had their *magical kiss*!

SOFIA'S APARTMENT, KITCHEN—EVENING

Sofia was preparing dinner when the phone rang. Jessie was calling.

Jessie was Sofia's dearest family friend in America but acted more like her mom. She treated Sofia like her own daughter and Nick like her grandchild. Jessie had known Sofia since she immigrated to the Unites States and helped Sofia raise Nick throughout his early childhood years up to the present day.

She was always ready to do anything for them. Jessie was a single, independent, strong, and very well-established woman. She lived on her own with a dog named Charlie in a beautiful house in Northern California. She always had high-profile jobs, but she retired early to manage her physical condition as she was afflicted with multiple sclerosis. Despite her physical limitations and use of a wheelchair, there was hardly anything that she couldn't do—or figure out how to get done. Jessie was in her late fifties and was an attractive woman with short light-brown hair, blue eyes, and fair skin.

Jessie always believed in Sofia and had faith in her. But at the same time she worried about Sofia's recent web series project because Sofia had taken out a $20,000 loan from the bank and was investing the majority of this money in her new project. Jessie was very concerned about this decision, and although she lived in Northern California, they communicated almost every day over the phone.

"Hi, sweetheart. I didn't hear from you the last couple of days, and I was wondering if everything was OK with you and Nick."

"Hi, Jessie. We're fine. Sorry, I was so busy the last few days with work and everything else, I didn't have a chance to call you."

"Honey, I was thinking about the loan that you took from the bank. Twenty thousand dollars is a lot of money. I know you work very hard, and I believe in you, but these web series scare me a little bit. Plus, you've got other expenses and responsibilities."

"I know, Jess…please don't worry about it. I'm working really hard to make it, and sometimes you need to take risks in life. Fear doesn't help you to accomplish your dreams. I want to do what I love because I believe I can. By the way, I actually have something to tell you."

"What is it? Are you all right?"

"Oh, yes, everything is OK. I just…I finally decided to date and…uh…I met a wonderful man, and I like him a lot."

Sofia was cutting veggies and was preparing soup at the same time.

"Oh, honey…that's fantastic news! I'm so happy for you. It's about time that you got out to have a little fun for yourself. Nick is already grown up, and he doesn't need you as much as he did when he was little. Now it's time for you! Tell me, who is he? Where did you guys meet? I am so excited…I can't wait to hear all about him." Jessie sounded very happy, and she had wanted Sofia to find a companion for a long time.

"Well, uh…his name is Marco…" Sofia was so animated while telling Jessie everything about Marco.

THEATER—DAY

Sofia and Katarina were shooting one of their episodes in the theater. The scene showed an actual performance by Sofia and Katarina playing with other actors. They were doing one of Shakespeare's plays, *Romeo and Juliet*. Abruptly, the phone rang, and everyone stopped. Sofia picked up the phone, and it was Marco.

"Marco..." she said very softly.

"Yes, Sofia...this is me...Marco." He replied softly too.

After a little pause, they both started laughing.

"You sound very romantic! Are you and Nick available tomorrow all day? I have a surprise for both of you."

"Yes, we are. What is it? Please...tell me what you're planning."

"It's a *surprise*, OK? My driver will pick you both up tomorrow at noon—see you then. Enjoy your shooting."

"Thanks. See you tomorrow." Sofia's eyes were sparkling with happiness.

STAPLES CENTER—DAY

Everyone was watching the Lakers vs. Cleveland game. Sofia, Marco, and Nick were sitting together and enjoying the game. This was Nick's first time being at Staples Center and watching a game live. He was so excited to be at the game where he could see his idol, LeBron James. A time-out was called.

"Nick, are you enjoying the game?" Marco asked.

"Of course. This is awesome! I love it! LeBron is the best. I'm so excited to be here." Nick was so cheerful and content.

"I'm glad you're having fun, and I hope your mom enjoys it." Marco looked at Sofia with a warm smile and touched her hand. "I love LeBron too. You're absolutely right, Nick. He is the king!"

"Yay! My mom is a Golden State Warriors fan, and she thinks Stephen Curry is the best. She's not into LeBron at all."

"That's fine. The Warriors are a great team too. But Cleveland is better..." Marco and Nick both laughed. Then Nick looked at his mom to see how she was reacting. Sofia was smiling, and she was happy that Nick and Marco were getting along well with each other: talking, interacting, and joking about things. They were both eating hot dogs and drinking sodas. All of these past years, Sofia had never let any men close to her son—she was very protective of him. This was a big step for her to let a man into her and her son's lives, and she felt blessed that she had met the man of her dreams. Marco put his hand on Sofia's shoulder, kissed her, and hugged her while watching the game. Marco enjoyed watching Nick's reaction to the game. He would jump up and cheer for LeBron.

BASKETBALL COURT—DAY

Marco, Sofia, and Nick were at a basketball court. Marco and Nick were playing basketball. Then Sofia joined them, and they were all having fun together. Sofia and Nick teamed up against Marco. Sofia tried to take the basketball from Marco, but Marco tripped and fell down, and Sofia fell on top of him. Then Nick tried to grab the basketball from Marco. They were all laughing lying down on the floor. After they were done playing basketball, Marco took them both to the store, and he bought LeBron James basketball shoes for Nick. Nick was more than thrilled with having LeBron's shoes in red. After shopping, they all went and enjoyed dinner together.

Marco's presence in Nick's life was creating many meaningful and significant moments and memories, and Sofia greatly appreciated it.

KATARINA'S HOUSE—EVENING

Sofia was dropping off Nick at Katarina's for a sleepover with Katarina's children. Katarina opened the door.

"Hi, guys! Come in. Nick, the boys are waiting for you. They're so excited."

Nick didn't even say hi and instead rushed in to see his friends with his knapsack still on his back. Sofia said, "Love you honey."

And Nick yelled from another room, "Love you too, Mom."

"Thank you, my friend, for letting Nick stay over tonight!" Sofia told to Katarina.

"Go…go, relax, and enjoy your time with Marco," Katarina responded with a joy. Then she grabbed Sofia and gave her a big hug.

THE ADAMS CLUB, HALLWAY—NIGHT

Sofia and Marco had just gotten off the elevator on the twelfth floor and were walking down the hallway.

"Marco, where are you taking me?" asked Sofia.

"I want to show you something. We're going up to the roof."

Marco reached one of the doors, got a key card out of his pocket, and inserted it into the lock. Sofia was confused because she thought they were going upstairs to the roof, but suddenly Marco opened the door, and they entered an apartment where, on a table, there was a bottle of French champagne; a fruit platter with strawberries, blackberries, and pineapple; and a beautiful vase of dark reddish-purple roses. The apartment had a gorgeous view of Los Angeles, and Sofia loved the place.

"Marco, this is amazing! What a lovely place. Do you stay here often?"

"Yes, if I work late, then I stay here overnight. I've been a member of this club for so many years and I really like being here too. The city mood is full of life and makes me feel energetic and happy."

Sofia went over to the roses and sniffed them. "Oh, Marco, these roses are just beautiful."

Marco embraced Sofia and kissed her. "*You are beautiful!* You bring me so much happiness. You're so, so sweet. You know, I compare you to a hummingbird because you're little, very curious, and always moving. Sometimes I think you're nervous or afraid of something, but you're just my little hummingbird." Sofia was speechless and still…Marco began kissing and embracing Sofia. They were very affectionate and passionate, full of gentle intimacy and overwhelming emotions.

Two Weeks Later

SOFIA'S APARTMENT, BATHROOM — EARLY MORNING

Sofia was sitting on the toilet and was in severe pain. She was even having a hard time getting up to get her phone. She needed help, but she didn't want to scare her son, Nick. Nick was in his room, still sleeping. Sofia finally got up, pulled her pajamas up, washed her hands and face, and checked herself in the mirror. She looked sick. She went to her bedroom and grabbed her phone. She couldn't walk straight. Sofia called Katarina.

"Sofia? Is everything OK?" It was 7:00 a.m. on a Saturday morning, and Katarina had not been expecting a phone call from Sofia that early.

"Kat…I'm in really bad pain. I need you…I need to go to the emergency room…please come." Sofia sounded desperate and in agony.

"Oh my God…I'm coming right now."

COMMUNITY GENERAL HOSPITAL, URGENT CARE—MORNING

Katarina was pushing Sofia in a wheelchair because she had no strength to walk. Katarina took her inside the building and straight to the door where a nurse took Sofia in.

"I will take her from here," the nurse said.

"Don't worry, Sofia…You'll be fine. I'll be waiting right here for you."

Sofia just nodded.

COMMUNITY GENERAL HOSPITAL, EXAM ROOM—SAME MORNING

Sofia was inside the exam room sitting on the exam table, and the doctor was sitting across from Sofia. The female doctor asked, "So what's going on? You said you're in pain."

"Yes, this morning when I went to the bathroom, I could hardly pee. It's burning inside of me, and it's very, very painful. The burning and itching started a few days ago, and I thought I had a vaginal yeast infection, so I used a three-day cream treatment. But nothing has changed, and the pain has gotten even worse."

"OK, let me examine you, and we'll also get a urine sample and send it to the lab to see if there is anything else going on. The nurse will give you a painkiller now, so you'll feel a little bit better shortly," the doctor said.

"OK." Sofia sighed. She was very concerned and very uncomfortable.

Shortly after, Sofia walked into the waiting room where Katarina was waiting impatiently. Katarina got up and rushed to Sofia, who looked very tired. Katarina was holding a coffee cup. "Sofia, tell me. What happened? What did the doctor say? What did this man do to you?"

"Nothing…no…Marco didn't do anything. I just…I have a bladder infection and a vaginal yeast infection too. I have to pick up a couple of medications and then everything will be fine." Sofia and Katarina began walking together in the hallway toward the pharmacy while talking. Katarina was sipping her coffee aggressively. "This is very painful. I've never had a bladder infection before. I feel awful, Kat. The doctor said that when you start a new relationship, especially if you haven't had a partner for a long time, this kind of thing could happen. I have to get used to his 'flora.'"

Katarina's tone of voice was serious but loving and a little comedic. "Sofia…that is crazy, but at the same time it's very true. You haven't been with a man for a quite a long time." Katarina was very direct. "You guys need to slow down. Maybe you did too much!" Katarina used her sense of humor and drank her coffee, and they continued walking.

"No…we just, oh no…we were together just a few times. But the last time it was…maybe you're right, it was too much." Sofia was a little embarrassed saying that.

Katarina looked at Sofia and started laughing. "He wore you out!"

Sofia paused a little, and then she cracked up too.

COMMUNITY GENERAL PHARMACY— SAME MORNING

Sofia was waiting to pick up her medication from the pharmacist at the counter. Katarina was standing next to her. "Are you going to tell Marco about this?"

"No, I don't want him to worry about it because he's leaving tomorrow for a few days for a business trip and I'm leaving this week too. Nick's school is over, and I'm driving him up to Northern California to spend the summer with Jessie and his friends. He misses living up there, and he can't wait to go. Actually, this will be the first time he'll be there without me. Let's see how he handles it. He needs to be more independent. And this way I can focus on our production, and I'll put more time into it. I've got so much to do. Kat, I am so blessed I have you in my life. Thank you for everything. For your love."

"Stop it now. I am always here for you. Remember, we are sisters." Katarina put her hand on Sofia's shoulder and hugged her.

NORTHERN CALIFORNIA, JESSIE'S HOUSE—DAY

Sofia and Nick got out of the car, grabbed some bags, and headed to the front door. Nick was running and screaming with excitement and couldn't wait to get in. He opened the door and saw Jessie was waiting impatiently for both of them. Charlie (a golden retriever and Lab mix), Jessie's dog, was sitting right next to her, and he was also very excited to see Nick and Sofia. He was thirteen years old, like Nick, but still acted like a puppy when everyone came home. Nick hugged Jessie quickly and ran straight to the kitchen because he knew that Jessie always made special treats for him. Nick started devouring the chocolate chip cookies, still warm from the oven, that Jessie had put out for him. Sofia finally got through the door and gave Jessie a huge hug and kiss. Sofia said, "Missed you," while hugging her. Sofia loved

Jessie very much, and Jessie loved them both like her own. She didn't have anyone else but them.

JESSIE'S HOUSE, KITCHEN—EVENING

Nick was searching again for something special in the kitchen. It was dinnertime, and Sofia was helping Jessie set the table in the dining room. Despite being in a wheelchair, Jessie was preparing dinner and was a great cook. She gave Sofia some dishes and napkins to put on the table.

"Jessie, what are we having for dinner?" Nick asked.

"Chicken, pilaf, and zucchini," Jessie replied.

"I don't like zucchini," Nick said.

"Do you want dessert?"

"What's for dessert?"

"I made brownies for you, so if you want them, you can have them after you eat the zucchini."

"OK…" Nick agreed. Although he didn't want to eat zucchini, he loved Jessie's brownies!

Jessie, Sofia, and Nick sat down at the table and started having dinner together. Sofia poured wine for Jessie and herself. Jessie loved wine, but Sofia only drank occasionally—and usually with Jessie. Sofia made a toast: "This toast is for the most loving and amazing woman in this world! Thank you for this delicious dinner and for everything you do for us. We love you so much!"

"Oh, honey…I love you both, too, and I'm happy you're here. I hope Nick isn't gonna drive me crazy this summer." Jessie looked at Nick.

Nick was quiet at first, and then he started singing the song "Crazy" by Patsy Cline. He said, "Of course, I'm gonna drive you crazy… That's my job!"

Jessie and Nick started laughing. Sofia shook her head, sipped her wine, and smiled. Nick and Jessie were really good friends. They did things together and had their secrets; their relationship was beautiful. Nick helped Jessie a lot, doing chores outside in the garden and inside the house. They got along very well, and Nick was very warm and loving to Jessie. She was like a real grandma to him.

After dinner Sofia helped Jessie clean up. Sofia was washing dishes in the sink, and Jessie was next to Sofia in her wheelchair, drying the dishes.

"Honey, how do you feel about your infection? Is it still painful? How long are you going to take the meds?"

"Now I feel better. It's getting better every day. I need to take the pills for another three days. Then I'll be fine."

"I think it'll be a good idea if you guys protect yourselves and take a little break. You need to be healed before anything more occurs."

"I know, I know. I'll be fine." Sofia was still washing dishes and wanted to change the subject. Jessie kept drying the dishes.

"Absolutely, you'll be fine. These kinds of things happen. How's Marco? Does he know about it?"

"No, he doesn't. I didn't tell him. He was going away, and I was coming here, so I'll tell him when I get back."

"Good." Jessie paused briefly before she said, "Marco seems like a very charming and nice gentleman. He treats you very well, and I'm so happy for you, sweetheart! You're a really special woman, and you deserve happiness after all of these years." Then Jessie took some dishes away.

JESSIE'S HOUSE, FAMILY ROOM—EVENING

Jessie was sitting on her recliner, and Sofia was sitting in Jessie's wheelchair next to her. They were having tea and a cozy conversation together.

"I think I'm falling in love with Marco. I have such strong feelings for him. I've never felt this way before. I'm very passionate with him, and he's also very affectionate, sweet, and wonderful to me. Nick likes him a lot, and they get along well. And Nick is so different now since Marco showed up in our lives. He's always happy when I'm going out with Marco, and he seems more confident as a young man just having a male role model in his life. I feel like it's a fairy-tale story."

"That is *so great*! Have you expressed your feelings to Marco?" Jessie asked with a smile.

"What do you mean? I haven't told him that I am falling in love with him, if that's what you're asking," Sofia replied.

"Why not?" Jessie asked again.

"Why doesn't he say it? He hasn't said anything yet. I want him to say it first." Sofia chuckled and kept drinking her tea.

"In relationships like this, there is no first or second. Who says 'I love you' first doesn't matter. You two aren't in high school anymore! If you have those true feelings, then you should tell him. He'll be thrilled to hear that from you. I know you had a heartbreak before and you're trying to protect yourself, but that was a long time ago, Sofia. Now you're a grown woman, and it's time to open your heart and tell him."

There was a little pause, and then Sofia said, "I think you're absolutely right! Yes…I will. Why not? I love him."

Sofia smiled and took a moment to collect her thoughts. "I truly do love him."

JESSIE'S HOUSE, FRONT FOYER—MORNING

Sofia was packed and saying goodbye to Jessie and Nick. She hugged both of them. "Nick, take care of Jessie. Now you are the man of the house. And be good, OK? I love you." Sofia kissed and hugged Nick.

"OK, Mom, I'll be good…love you too!" Nick ran next door to the neighbor's house to play with his friends. He was so happy to stay with Jessie.

"Don't worry, honey, he'll be fine. He's happy here, you know. Go. Focus on your work, and enjoy your summer. Love you!"

Sofia walked out the door.

LOS ANGELES AIRPORT—DAY

In front of the airport at the passenger pickup area, Marco was back from his business trip and was walking to the car where his driver was waiting. He got in the car, and his phone rang. It was Sofia.

"Hummingbird…I miss you! How are you?"

"Marco!" Sofia loved saying Marco's name. She said it so lovingly that Marco loved hearing it. "I miss you too! How was your flight?"

"It was peaceful! I just landed a few minutes ago, and I'm heading home. I'll rest a little, get ready, and then come over tonight. I can't wait to see you and have whatever delightful meal you're making today. Actually, this is my first time coming to your place!"

"I know…I can't wait to see you too. OK, I'll let you go. I'm busy cooking!"

"What are you making?"

"It's a surprise, just come hungry! See you tonight. Bye."

Sofia hung up the phone. Marco was sitting in the car and looked very happy.

SOFIA'S APARTMENT, DINING ROOM—EVENING

Sofia made traditional Polish dishes. She set the table beautifully with decorations, flowers, and candles. The apartment looked gorgeous, especially the dinner table. The bell rang, and Sofia opened the door.

"Hi," Marco said. He was holding beautiful purple and white roses. He entered the room and kissed Sofia.

Sofia kissed him back, took the roses, and welcomed him into her apartment. "These roses are gorgeous, Marco. Thank you."

"You look gorgeous!" Marco said.

Sofia was stylishly dressed, and Marco looked very handsome and sharp. They both were heading toward the kitchen. Marco was looking around and was enjoying the place very much. The apartment was small but very cozy. He was checking the living room and dining room and saw a piano in the corner of the living room.

"Your apartment is beautiful. It feels like a real home. I see your piano here. Would you play for me later?"

Even though Marco was very wealthy, he didn't have one particular place that he called home. He bought and sold properties, houses, and buildings, but he never stayed at one place for very long. Sofia was already in the kitchen putting the roses into a vase.

"Thank you, Marco! I like my place too. I'm so lucky that I found it. And sure, I can play piano after dinner if you'd like."

Marco was checking Sofia's dishes on the table. He walked into the kitchen and saw more things on the kitchen counter. He was so impressed and couldn't wait to start tasting Sofia's dishes. He saw pierogis, filled dumplings that were beautifully spread on a plate in the kitchen; placki ziemniaczane, pancakes made with potatoes; and other appetizers that Sofia had made. Marco started tasting the appetizers while Sofia put the main hot dish on the table; she had made golabki, traditional stuffed cabbage rolls.

"Wow…Sofia! Everything looks so beautiful and delicious." Marco was eating and enjoying everything. "Oh my God, you are the best cook ever. *You are amazing!*" Marco was thrilled about everything Sofia had done to welcome him to her home.

"Thank you, Marco! I'm so happy," Sofia replied.

"No one has ever cooked for me like this…maybe only my grandmother," Marco said, and they both laughed. "She was a very good cook, but *you are the best!*"

"Really?" Sofia smiled. "Thank you! OK, then… dinner is ready. Let's sit down and enjoy it." They both grabbed their drinks and sat down at the table. Then they brought their glasses together and said in unison, "Cheers!"

Marco and Sofia had finished eating dinner, and they were sitting together at the piano in the living room. Sofia was trying to teach Marco *Moonlight Sonata* by

Beethoven. Marco was playing the first part slowly, and he looked very happy. He was thrilled about everything that Sofia did. He loved piano and had always dreamed of learning how to play it. But he never pursued it because he was so consumed with his real estate business.

"You are my beautiful hummingbird. You bring me *so much* happiness. Thank you for making this evening so special."

While they were sitting at the piano, Marco started kissing Sofia slowly. He hugged her gently, and they both got very affectionate with each other.

SOFIA'S APARTMENT— THE NEXT MORNING, 6:30 A.M.

Marco was sleeping, and Sofia was getting up from the bed very quietly. She looked sick and in pain. She went to the bathroom and dressed very quickly. She didn't want to wake up Marco. She was feeling horrible, so she got her car key and drove her car out from the garage. She headed to the hospital.

COMMUNITY GENERAL HOSPITAL, URGENT CARE EXAM ROOM— SAME MORNING

Sofia was sitting across from the doctor. The female doctor was looking at the computer. Then she looked up at Sofia.

"We've checked your lab results. The reason for the painful urination that you are having is a persistent vaginal infection, which could have been caused by the antibiotics that you were taking for your bladder infection. Unfortunately it can happen. This infection can be very painful and irritating. I'll prescribe you some meds that can help you with the pain and infection. The pain should go away in a few hours, and in a few days, you should be infection free."

"Oh, no…I can't believe this." Sofia was so frustrated and upset.

"I'm sorry. I know it is painful. If you don't feel well in a few days, you should come back, and we'll do another test. But I think you should be fine."

"OK, thank you." Sofia looked very pale and tired.

SOFIA'S APARTMENT, BEDROOM—SAME MORNING

Marco woke up and checked his phone. It was 9:00 a.m. He looked around and didn't see Sofia. He called out, "Sofia…Sofia…" Then he got up, grabbed his pants and put them on, went to the bathroom, finished dressing, and came out. By the time he walked into the kitchen, he had figured out that Sofia wasn't home. He opened the refrigerator and took out some yogurt and bread. He put a couple of slices of bread in the toaster, sat down at the kitchen table, and started eating the yogurt. Finally, he took his phone out and called Sofia. She walked into the apartment at that moment and went straight to the kitchen. She was so down and looked very fragile.

"Where have you been? Where did you go?"

"I woke up really early and I didn't feel well, so I went to urgent care. I have another vaginal infection caused by the antibiotics that I was taking for the bladder infection that I had before."

"Oh no, Sofia. I am so sorry." Marco got up and embraced her. "Why didn't you leave me a note that you were going to the hospital? Or you should have texted me. I didn't know where you were, and I was worried about you."

"I'm sorry. I was rushing, and it was so early, and I was in pain. I thought that I'd be back before you woke up. How long have you been up?"

"Maybe just half an hour."

"Why didn't you call me when you woke up?"

"I thought you went to the store to pick up something. How do you feel now? What else did the doctor say?"

"I'm OK now—just weak and tired. The doctor didn't say anything else. I just need to take meds for the infection, and everything should be fine."

Marco was very warm with Sofia. He tried to comfort her by hugging her, but at the same time, he was thinking that he had to go. Sofia just wanted to go to bed and rest.

"I have to go. You know that I have some business meetings this morning, so you just rest. If you need anything, call me."

"OK, I will." Marco kissed Sofia goodbye and walked out the door.

Two Weeks Later

BEVERLY HILLS, MARCO'S HOUSE—DAY

Marco was in the hallway, grabbing his phone and wallet from a cabinet. He walked out of the house and got into his Ferrari. He was dressed up in a business suit and looked very corporate. He was going to meet a new client who was offering a half-billion-dollar business contract deal. Marco was driving when his phone rang. Marco's assistant, Scott, was calling. Scott was in his early to mid-thirties.

"Yes, Scott…how's everything?" Marco sounded very serious and focused. Although Scott worked for Marco and liked him as a boss, he was sometimes intimidated by him. Marco had a very bad temper at work, and at times, he made his employees cry.

"Hi, Marco. The client called, and he'll be here in about twenty minutes. I've got all the documents ready for you. You're all set."

"Wonderful, Scott! Doesn't it feel fantastic to sign a deal for a half-billion dollars? What a contract and what an accomplishment!" Marco's ego was so high, and he sounded extremely proud of himself. He liked to be a winner.

"Absolutely, Boss!" Scott sounded happy, but he was still a little bit cautious.

"I'll be there in five minutes. Bye, Scott." As Marco was driving, he put rap music on and got excited.

MARCO'S OFFICE, CONFERENCE ROOM—SAME DAY

Marco, his assistant, and three other people were in the room. They were signing the papers, shaking one another's hands, and getting ready to leave the place. Marco stayed in the room. His assistant, Scott, walked out of the room with the clients. Marco was sitting at the table and took a moment to digest his happiness from this deal. He picked up the phone and called Sofia. Sofia was in the store buying a cake for Marco's birthday. They were going to celebrate his birthday in the evening. When Sofia's phone rang, she picked it up from her purse.

"Marco, how are you? How did everything go today?"

"Hummingbird...everything is just perfect! The king had a very successful business meeting." Marco liked calling himself a king and the winner. "But most importantly, I can't wait to see you tonight. Where are you?" Sofia was chuckling about Marco calling himself a king. She didn't take it seriously.

"I can't wait to see you too. I'm happy about your business accomplishment—congratulations! I'm at the store right now getting a birthday cake for the 'king.'" Sofia chuckled.

"Wow...what kind of cake? I'm already hungry."

"I'm not telling you."

"OK. I'm going to the club for a workout. I'll see you tonight."

"See you, bye."

MARCO'S HOUSE—MIDNIGHT, AFTER BIRTHDAY DINNER

Marco opened the house door, and they both walked in. It was late. They had just finished his birthday dinner and were back home. They both went straight to the bedroom. While Marco was in the bathroom, Sofia quietly took from her purse a gift that she had made for him and quickly put it on his pillow. The gift was printed on special paper rolled up like a diploma with a ribbon wrapped around it; it was a poem that Sofia had written for Marco. Then she went to the kitchen, opened the cake box, placed the cake on a plate, put a candle in it, and brought it back to the bedroom. She lit the candle and turned the lights off. Marco came out of the bathroom and approached Sofia.

"Wow! This cake looks *super*! Sofia, thank you." Marco blew out the candle and made a wish. They tried the cake together. "This is *delicious*...mmmm...I love it!" Marco said.

"It is really, really good!" Sofia agreed.

"I'm having an amazing birthday with you. I'm so happy that you're with me and I have you in my life. You made this night so special." Marco kissed Sofia. Then he noticed the rolled-up paper with a beautiful ribbon wrapped around it. "What is that?" Marco asked.

"That...is a surprise. It's your birthday gift. Open it."

Marco was exuberant and began untying the ribbon. He unrolled the paper and saw that it was a poem Sofia had written for him. Marco read it and was touched, but he wanted Sofia to read it out loud in her sweet voice.

"This is a beautiful poem. You wrote this? Please... read it to me."

"OK." Sofia started reading it:

I have wrapped my heart with so much passion
And put it in a sacred box for you
I have kissed every part of your body and left the
Scent of love within
I have touched your sweet lips so gently that it made
Me feel free and divine
Now I can speak so proudly because every cell of my
Body wants to dance.

"You wrote this poem for me?" Marco asked.

Sofia nodded her head.

"This is beautiful...*Wow*! Thank you! You are *beautiful*!"

Marco kissed Sofia with passion and embraced her, and Sofia kissed him back.

Two Days Later

Sofia was driving her car, and she looked awful while driving. She was getting a call from Maddie. She answered the call.

"Maddie..." Sofia couldn't even speak properly because she was in pain.

"Sofia, what's going on? I got your message. You sound terrible. Are you driving? Where are you?" Maddie was very nervous.

"Sorry, Maddie, for bothering you about my issues. But I'm going to the emergency room. I woke up this morning, and I couldn't pee again. I feel like I am going to explode. I don't know what's going on. I've noticed the last couple of days that I was peeing slowly and needed to push really hard. I didn't want to scare Jessie by calling her this morning. Besides, she can't do anything from there. I'm in terrible pain, Maddie..."

"Oh my God, Sofia…you are crazy! You should have called me, and I would have picked you up and taken you to the emergency room." Maddie was very concerned and was worried about Sofia's condition. "How are you even driving? That's dangerous! Oh, Sofia, I can't believe this. Please drive carefully. Which hospital are you going to? I'm coming right now."

"I'm going to Community General. Please, you don't need to come. I'll be fine. I'll call you later."

"Don't tell me what to do. I'll be there soon." Maddie was getting mad.

They both hung up the phone. Sofia was getting worse and was in serious pain, but she kept driving.

COMMUNITY GENERAL HOSPITAL, EMERGENCY ROOM—DAY

Sofia was rushing through the emergency room. She couldn't even stand on her feet anymore and collapsed in front of the emergency desk. She started screaming, "Help, help me…Please help me!"

Nurses quickly came out from the other doors. One brought a wheelchair, and they tried to put her in it. At the same time, one of the nurses asked Sofia, "What's wrong? Where do you have pain?

"I can't pee! I'm dying..." Sofia couldn't say anything more. "Please help me..."

"OK. When was the last time you peed?"

Sofia couldn't even respond to the nurse, and she was hardly breathing. "I don't remember..."

All three nurses rushed to take Sofia directly to an exam room where they could help her. They knew that this could be very dangerous. Even though Sofia was screaming loudly, they were able to get her to lie down on the exam table. The nurses then proceeded to catheterize her to relieve the pressure on her bladder.

Maddie was sitting and waiting for Sofia to come out. After a while Sofia finally opened the door and started walking toward Maddie. Maddie, who was very nervous by now, got up and rushed to Sofia.

"Oh, Sofia, how are you? What did they say?"

Sofia looked devastated, frightened, and very down.

"They put a catheter in me because I couldn't pee. The doctor told me that if I came in a few minutes later, nothing could have helped me. It's so scary, Maddie. I don't know...why is this happening?"

Sofia burst into tears and got very emotional. Maddie was shocked and speechless. Maddie put her hand on

Sofia's shoulder, hugged her, and tried to comfort her as much as she could. A few minutes later, when Sofia had calmed down a little bit, they started walking together to the door.

Maddie felt so bad for Sofia, watching what she was going through. They came out from the emergency room and sat together on a little bench right in front of the ER. Sofia was exhausted from everything. Maddie sounded very concerned, upset, and angry.

"*I can't believe this*! I don't know what to say…I can't believe that you need a catheter, and you're going through something like this…this is crazy, Sofia! This is truly *crazy*! Why? What did the doctor say? Why is this happening? Maybe Marco has something, and he needs to get checked!"

"No. I talked to the doctor about that, too, but she said that it's nothing to do with him. She said because I had so many infections—a bladder infection and a yeast infection—and took so many antibiotics and medications, that this could have been the reason why I couldn't pee. My system completely shut down. They did a blood test and sent everything to the lab to make sure that there is nothing else going on."

"So what else did they say?" Maddie asked.

"The doctor said that I am healthy otherwise, and I don't have anything else. Even the doctor and the nurses looked surprised that I need a catheter." Sofia was totally lost.

"I still don't get it. You're a healthy young woman, but you need a catheter. Why? Because you had sex with your boyfriend? And because you had a few infections? I've never heard of anything like this in my entire life. A woman having sex with a partner and needing a catheter because she can't pee? What did you guys do? This sounds unbelievable…" Maddie was angry, but at the same time she laughed in disbelief.

Although Sofia was devastated, tired, and irritated, she stared at Maddie and, after a little pause, started laughing and crying. She thought that all of this was crazy. "I can't believe it either. I have never had any health issues or any of these types of problems with my ex or previous relationships. I've only had a couple of serious ones, but I was always fine."

"For me it feels like you have an allergic reaction to Marco!"

Sofia smiled. "No. Actually, the doctor said that Marco introduced his flora to me, and my system is reacting adversely to it. So it will take some time for me to get used to that. That's why these types of infections sometimes happen. And because of these infections, now I need a catheter."

Maddie was shaking her head. She rolled her eyes and got up from the bench. "*Wow…this is unbelievable.* OK, you stay here, and I'll go get the car. Give me your car key."

Sofia handed her car key to Maddie, and Maddie walked to the parking lot to get her car. Sofia stayed on the bench by herself.

SOFIA'S APARTMENT, KITCHEN—EVENING

Maddie was making tea for Sofia and herself. Sofia was lying down on the couch, very pale and tired. She had a blanket over her, and Maddie brought a teacup over and handed it to her. Maddie got her own tea and sat next to Sofia.

"Maddie, I can't thank you enough for being so wonderful and loving. I was going to call Jessie this morning, but then I asked myself 'What could she do?' Nothing. And she would have gone crazy. I'll call her later and explain everything."

"What about Marco? Are you going to call him and tell him what happened? That's what you should do. He's part of this, and he should be here with you and help you through this."

"I know. He's out of town on a business trip for a few days, so I'll call him later. I don't want to stress him out about this, and honestly, I don't really want him here right now while I have this catheter. It's so embarrassing...I feel awful..." Sofia got very emotional, and she was all in tears. "I would never ever have imagined that I would need a catheter to pee just because I was with Marco! What is this all about?" Sofia was devastated, and Maddie hugged her, trying to comfort her. "It's OK. I can take care of myself."

"Sofia, you'll be fine. Please remember, the doctors are saying that you're a healthy woman. This will go away soon. Sometimes things happen for a reason, and even though we don't know what that reason is right now, I'm sure that something beautiful is gonna happen in your life, and you'll forget about all of this pain. You know that I love you, and I'm here for you. But I think you should tell Marco about this sooner rather than later. He needs to be here next to you to comfort you and give you his love and attention. Because again, he's part of this, and if he cares about you, he needs to take care of you. This wouldn't have happened to you if he wasn't in your life. If he considers himself your boyfriend and he loves you, he should be concerned about your condition and be here. That's what I think is important for a good, successful, and healthy relationship. So please, don't feel uncomfortable or embarrassed about this. This event will show you how much he loves and cares about you… and I'm sure he does."

"You're absolutely right. I'll tell him everything tonight." Sofia was drinking her tea and was very sad. "I have so much work to do. I was hoping that while Nick was away I would be able to focus on my project and dedicate more time to that. Katarina is out of town traveling with her kids for a couple of weeks so that actually makes me feel a little bit better, but I still need to work with my editor, and I have lots of other things to do. I can't go out…even if my manager calls me for an audition. What would I say? 'Sorry, I can't go because I have a catheter!' This is so crazy—it's unreal…"

"I agree…but remember, your health is more important than your work. You can tell your manager the truth, and she'll understand. It shouldn't be a problem. People get sick—we're all human beings. I would suggest that you do some meditation every day. It'll help you heal and recover faster. Think about yourself, and take care of your body first. This is your project now. You're strong, smart, and very organized, and once you're back to normal, you'll take care of everything else very quickly. When Katarina comes back, she'll understand everything and will be very supportive—don't worry."

"Of course, she will…although she'll go crazy… She won't believe this." Sofia sighed and stayed quiet. Maddie felt terrible for Sofia. She got up, picked up the teacups, and took them to the kitchen.

SOFIA'S APARTMENT BEDROOM— SAME DAY, 8:00 P.M.

Sofia was in the bathroom taking a shower. She came out of the shower and checked her catheter to make sure it was placed correctly before she went to bed. She put on her pj's, got into bed, took her phone, and started texting Marco.

"Marco, I hope you're having a productive trip! This morning after we spoke, I didn't feel well, so I drove to urgent care where I collapsed in pain due to an overextended bladder. They took care of me today, but I have to go back early tomorrow morning to see a urologist. I have a catheter now because I can't pee by myself. I'm sorry, I don't want to add more complications to your plate right now, but I can't hide this from you. I feel so bad for sharing my problems with you. Have a safe trip and talk to you soon. Sofia"

Sofia grabbed one of her favorite poetry books (Hafiz) and started reading it. She heard a beep on her phone and saw that she had a text from Marco.

"Dear Sofia, I'm sorry about all of this. I will call you soon—I'm still at the meeting."

Sofia put her phone and book away. She was sad but fighting back tears. She closed her eyes and fell asleep. She was still sleeping when the phone started ringing. She woke up suddenly, grabbed her phone, and saw that Marco was calling.

"Marco…" Sofia answered the phone in a sleepy voice.

"Sofia, I can't believe that this is happening to you! This is crazy. I don't know what to say. When I get back, I'll go with you to see a doctor, and we can talk to the doctor together. What has the doctor said?"

"The doctor said that I don't have anything serious, and it's not really your fault. He said sometimes when you start a new relationship, these infections happen, and I have to get use to your flora slowly. Eventually I'll be fine."

"I've had a lot of relationships, and I've never encountered anything like this. This is unbelievable! Is there anything I can do for you? Do you need anything?"

"No, thank you. I'm fine, and I have everything I need. Maddie was here with me almost all day, and she helped me with a few things."

"OK, then…just rest and please take it easy. You'll be fine. You're very strong and healthy. I'll be out of town for another two days. I still have some very important meetings, but I'll be checking on you regularly. Have a good night and sweet dreams."

"Good night."

SOFIA'S APARTMENT, BEDROOM—2:00 A.M.

Sofia couldn't sleep, and she was in pain. She was moving in her bed and couldn't find a comfortable position. She got up slowly, feeling horrible. She looked terrible, went to the bathroom, emptied her catheter, took off her pj's, and took a shower. Then she came out and started walking back and forth because she couldn't sit. The catheter was bothering her, and she felt very itchy. She decided to meditate. She sat down on her bed slowly, closed her eyes, and in a few seconds, she burst out crying; she was distressed.

The next morning, it was 7:30 a.m., and Sofia was sitting on her bed, leaning against the wall and sleeping.

After having the conversation with Sofia, the next morning Marco decided to fly to Hawaii, where he stayed at one of the best beach resorts and spent the day with a scuba diving instructor, learning how to dive. Then Marco enjoyed some suntanning, food and drinks on a yacht, and a relaxing massage. He was indulging himself and had a delightful few days in Hawaii.

Four Days Later

PUBLIC PARK—MORNING

Sofia was walking in the park while wearing her catheter. She looked tired, weak, and sad. She received a phone call from Jessie.

"Hi, Jessie."

"Hi, honey. I'm thinking about you, and I'm very worried. How are you today? Do you feel any better?"

"I'm OK. I'm at the park, just walking…enjoying nature, and trying to stay positive." Sofia quickly got very sad and could not hold her tears. She kneeled down on the ground and started crying out loud. "This is so hard, Jess. I feel awful…I can't wait another three days to get it out."

In a very concerned and loving voice, Jessie said, "Oh, honey, I'm just devastated knowing what you're going through. Please, you have to stay positive. You're strong and healthy; you know that. You just need another few days, and the doctor will remove it. I'm glad that

Nick is with me, and he's not watching what you're going through. He would have been so heartbroken, knowing how much this boy loves you."

"I know…" Sofia calmed down a little bit. "Even my parents don't know anything about this. I don't want them to worry about me."

"Absolutely not. Don't tell them—you don't need to. I'm here for you. I wish I could do more. Is there anything you need? I ordered some things online, and everything will be delivered today, so please make sure that you'll be home later this afternoon."

"Oh no…you shouldn't have done that. I have everything I need, but thanks so much. You do so much for Nick and me…I love you!"

"It's nothing, sweetheart. I love you, too, and I want you to stay strong and happy. You'll get through this, and everything will be fine. I'm here for you."

"Thank you."

"Is Marco back? Have you heard from him?"

"No, I haven't spoken with him for four days. It's good that he's gone because I really don't want anyone around me right now." Although Sofia said this, in her heart she was sad that Marco hadn't called to check on her. "I just want peace and harmony."

"I understand, sweetie. I'm sure that he'll call you when he gets back." Jessie was pissed off but didn't want to say anything to hurt Sofia's feelings even more. "OK, honey, please go home and rest. Don't do anything taxing, and stay focused on getting better. Everything will be just fine. You'll be back to normal soon. Nick is great, and he's happy here, so don't worry about him either. Call me if you need anything. I love you."

"Thank you, Jessie. I love you so much!"

Jessie hung up the phone. She was so mad at Marco, and she angrily said out loud, "That son of a bitch." She pushed her wheelchair button so hard that the button popped off the controller and the wheelchair started making weird noses. Jessie started screaming, "Nick… Nick!"

Two Days Later

GROCERY STORE—DAY

Sofia was doing her grocery shopping and pushing her cart through the vegetable section. She was picking up a few things and discreetly checking her catheter to make sure that it was in place. She was startled by her phone ringing. Katarina, who had returned from traveling with her family, was calling from her car. She didn't know anything about Sofia's condition.

"Katarina…I missed you!" Sofia was happy to hear Katarina's voice. "How are you?"

"I miss you more, my Sofia. We are finally back and very tired. How are you doing? I was thinking about you the whole time."

"I hope you guys had a fantastic time on the East Coast and that the kids are happy."

"We did. The kids had an awesome time. It was really good, but I'm glad that we're back. I'll tell you more when I see you. How is everything with you?"

"Don't ask…OK, long story short…please don't be scared, but I have a catheter because I can't pee by myself."

When Katarina heard this, she slammed on the breaks and stopped her car in the middle of the street. She almost got into a car accident, then pulled over to the curb.

"*What the hell?*" Katarina yelled very loudly, and Sofia heard tires screeching.

"Kat, are you OK?"

"Yes, I'm OK, but what the hell is going on with you? What did this man, *Marco*, do to you? Don't even let him touch you," she said in a serious and angry voice. "*I want to kill him.*"

"Kat, please calm down. Marco didn't do anything. It's not really his fault, I mean…" Sofia was continuing to shop while talking.

"What do you mean it's not his fault? You were a healthy woman with no physical issues, and now you have a catheter and can't pee! Whose fault is it then? You had sex with him. Maybe he has some kind of bacteria and he needs to get a checkup." When Katarina talked about Marco, she was very dramatic and emotional, but at the same time, she had this beautiful comedic essence in her voice that made the conversation a little bit lighter.

"Kat, Marco told me he already got checked out, and he's willing to come with me to see my doctor and talk to her. But my doctor said that because this was a new relationship and I got so many infections in the beginning, that's why I'm having this problem now. I have to get used to him, and then everything will be fine."

"*Used to him?* I can't believe this…Oh my God…I want to kill him." Katarina was still sitting in her car.

"*No, don't kill him!*" Sofia replied softly. In the store a couple of ladies heard Sofia's conversation, and they both stared at her. Sofia looked back at them with a little smile. At the same time, Sofia felt that her catheter bag was filling up. She needed to hurry up and go home to empty it.

"Sofia, I want to die right now. What did he do to you?"

"Katarina! Please don't die!"

"I hate men…" Still angry, Katarina started driving her car.

"Kat, I have to run. My catheter bag is getting filled up, and I need to rush. I'll call you later."

"Of course…go…go…I'll see you soon!" Katarina hung up the phone. She was so angry. She screamed, "*Fuck!*"

Sofia was rushing out of the store. Her catheter bag was getting very heavy, and suddenly, the bag fell down almost on her foot. It hung while she walked quickly with two grocery bags in her hands. A couple of guys were walking toward the store. When they passed Sofia, they saw the catheter bag hanging above her foot. She quickly put the grocery bags on the ground, picked up the catheter bag, and reattached it to the strap on her leg. She ignored the guys watching her and continued walking away very quickly with her groceries. She was so embarrassed.

One Week Later

COMMUNITY GENERAL HOSPITAL, PATIENT ROOM—DAY

The nurse was preparing to remove Sofia's catheter, but before she did that, she put water through the catheter to fill up Sofia's bladder. Sofia looked very tired and irritated.

"I think I'm ready. I can't take this anymore. I feel like I want to go to the bathroom." Sofia's voice was very fragile and weak.

"OK, let me just take it out. Try and relax," the nurse said.

A few minutes later, Sofia was in the hospital bathroom, sitting on the toilet and trying to pee. She was devastated because her bladder was filled up, but she couldn't go! She tried to push but had no success. She called Jessie from the bathroom.

Sofia was crying. "Jessie…I can't pee. I am trying, but I can't do it."

Jessie was in the kitchen cooking. "Honey, just breathe…please breathe. You can do it. Let's breathe together." Jessie started rhythmic breathing by herself, inhaling and exhaling. "You can do it. Oh my God, you're making me feel like now I want to pee! You're stressed right now, Sof, and that's why you can't go. Turn the water on in the sink, and let it run. Sometimes the sound of running water helps. It also might help if you can get up and move around a little bit. Just relax honey."

"OK." Sofia got up, turned the water on, and started moving around the bathroom; she was broken and distraught. "I don't know what to do. I wanna pee so badly…" She burst out crying while pacing back and forth. "My bladder is so full, and I'm trying to push, but nothing's coming. Oh, God, help me." Sofia kept breathing. She was moving and pacing even though she was extremely uncomfortable and devastated. Her personality and style always had a little amusing lightness.

"Sofia, listen to me. This is all psychological. You just need to calm down. You need to relax, and you'll go—don't worry. Remember, there's nothing wrong with you. Everyone says you're healthy. Can you just go out and walk in the hallway a little bit? Or better yet, go to the cafeteria and get a big cup of *hot tea*…That might help you. Can you hold it for another ten or fifteen minutes? And even if you can't, who cares? You're in a hospital!"

"OK, I'll go out and will call you in a bit."

COMMUNITY GENERAL HOSPITAL, HALLWAY—SAME DAY

Sofia was walking in the hallway and was heading toward the cafeteria. She kept saying, "I want to pee by myself…I want to pee by myself." Then her phone rang. It was Marco.

"Hi, Marco…" Sofia sounded very sad.

"Please tell me that you peed."

"No, I couldn't. I'm walking in the hallway and hoping that I'll be able to go soon," Sofia responded in a weak voice.

"You will. You're strong and healthy—remember that. Go and get a big bottle of cold juice or water and drink it all. *Cold*, like ice water, is good for you. Do it now. Please trust me. It'll help you. And please breathe and relax. I promise you'll do it. I'll come and see you tonight—I miss you."

Sofia was in the cafeteria getting some drinks while talking to Marco on the phone.

"Marco, hold on a second please." Sofia turned to the cafeteria worker. "Hi, can I get a big cup of hot tea, please?"

"What? You're getting hot tea? I said ice water or cold juice, not hot!" Marco said it loudly over the phone.

"Yes, Marco, you're right." Then Sofia called to the cafeteria worker, "Excuse me, can I get a bottle of cold water and orange juice?" Sofia looked and sounded exhausted.

The cafeteria worker was confused and sounded a little angry. She asked rudely, "So what do you want? Hot tea, a bottle of cold water, or orange juice?"

Sofia paused. Her eyes were full of tears, and she was very emotional. "I want *hot tea, iced water, and cold orange juice. Everything—and I want to pee too*!" Sofia tried to hold her tears in and then said, "I'm sorry for the confusion."

The lady understood that Sofia was not feeling well, and she changed her attitude radically. "Of course, I'll get them for you right away."

Marco was quiet. He felt Sofia's emotions over the phone.

"Marco, please don't come tonight. I'm not feeling well, and I'm tired and stressed, and I feel uncomfortable about you seeing me with this catheter."

"What do you mean uncomfortable? It's OK…I haven't seen you in a while, and I want to be there with you. I miss you, and I'm still coming. You'd better open the door! I don't want to stress you out now, so please go and try to pee. I know you can do it—I'll see you tonight."

SOFIA'S APARTMENT, LIVING ROOM—EVENING

Sofia was putting music on her phone, and Marco was sitting on the couch. *The Blue Danube*, a waltz by Strauss, started to play.

"Marco, come to me," Sofia said.

Marco got up and approached Sofia, and she started showing Marco how to waltz. "Now hold my hands straight. Yes, like that, and follow me. First with your left foot…one…then your right foot…good…then turn… nice. So remember, when you waltz with your partner, there is always a leader, in this case you, and a follower, in this case, me. The leader is responsible for guiding the couple. You make the step choices, and you direct me."

"Which means I'm your king." Marco chuckled and followed Sofia's directions.

Sofia smiled and said, "Yes, and I'm your queen!"

Marco was so happy. He loved everything he did with Sofia, and she looked happier just being with him. They continued dancing, but Sofia kept checking her catheter. Every time she did, Marco teased her and attempted to touch it too. Sofia pushed him away while they laughed and had fun.

"I love dancing with you. I could do it all night. I've never danced the waltz before. I didn't know how to. This is amazing. I'm getting better!" Marco was so excited.

"You are very good…You're actually a very talented man!" They kept dancing.

"I have to run…I'll be back. Keep practicing," Sofia said, and she ran to the bathroom. Marco decided to play the piano. He sat down and started practicing *Moonlight Sonata*, the piece that Sofia had taught him. Shortly after Sofia walked into the room and approached him from behind. When Marco finished the first part, Sofia kissed him on his neck and embraced him from behind.

"Yay…well done."

"No one in my life has ever suggested that I should try to learn how to play piano. I have two pianos at home because I love this instrument so much but I *never* believed I would be able to play it. And look at me after only a few short days with you. I'm so grateful to you that you made this magic happen." Marco smiled with happiness and kissed Sofia.

JESSIE'S HOUSE, BACKYARD— FOURTH OF JULY, DAY

Nick was running around the pool with Charlie, and they were jumping into the pool and swimming together. Jessie was having family and friends over, and they were outside barbecuing burgers, setting the picnic table, and getting ready for their Fourth of July celebration. Everyone was in a festive mood. Jessie received a call from Sofia.

"Hi, honey! Happy Fourth of July! Nick, come on, this is mommy. Talk to her."

Nick ran over, all wet, and picked up the phone. "Hi, Mommy—I miss you! Happy Fourth of July. How are you?"

"Sweetheart, I miss you too! Are you having fun today?"

"Yes, I'm swimming with Charlie, and I can't wait to have a burger. I have to run. I'm all wet. I love you! I'm giving the phone to Jessie…"

"OK…love you too!" Sofia sounded a little sad. She missed Nick, but she was happy that he wasn't seeing her in this condition.

"How are you feeling? Are you home?"

"I'm OK. Yes, I'm home…just resting," Sofia replied with a low-spirited voice.

"Is Marco coming tonight?"

"No. He went to his beach club to see his friends. They're going to celebrate Fourth of July together."

"Hmm…really?" Jessie's voice changed a little bit.

"He said he would love to have taken me but knew that I couldn't go in this condition. So that's OK. He needs to spend some time with his friends too." Sofia tried to defend Marco.

Jessie was holding her emotions in. She didn't want to light a fire between Marco and Sofia because she knew that Sofia loved him, and she didn't want to hurt her feelings. But Jessie was annoyed, and she lost her focus on the grill until a burger started to flare up. She backed up her wheelchair, and a family friend came over to help her.

"I understand, honey. You need to rest. I wish you were here with us, but right now the best thing for you is to be positive and take it easy because tomorrow you have another very important day. They'll remove your catheter, and you'll finally be free of it. So focus on that, and everything will be fine."

"Yes, I know. Plus my manager called me today, and I have a big audition tomorrow in the late afternoon for a feature-length movie. The role is for an Eastern European dance instructor."

"That's fantastic! I'm so happy for you! You'll be fine—don't worry. I'm sure they'll remove that catheter tomorrow, and then you'll go to your audition and nail it!" Jessie said in a very encouraging way.

"I hope so too. I'm studying the audition script and trying to stay motivated. OK, Jessie, please go and take care of your guests. Enjoy your day with everyone, and I'll talk to you tomorrow. I love you so much!"

"I love you too, honey. Talk to you tomorrow." Jessie hung up the phone. She was so upset about the situation that Sofia was in; she turned her wheelchair on and drove into the house.

BEACH CLUB—LATE AFTERNOON

Marco was enjoying his time with his friends. They were having drinks and food on the beach and were laughing and playing volleyball. It was getting late—almost 6:00 p.m.—and Marco was checking his watch. He was sitting on the sand close to the water and decided to call Sofia. Marco had two sides: sometimes he was very sweet and tender with Sofia, and sometimes he was very cold and sounded very formal, which annoyed her. That's when his ego was speaking.

"Sofia, how are you? Happy Fourth of July!"

"Happy Fourth of July to you too. Hope you're having fun with your friends over there."

"Oh, yeah, we had a good time, and now everyone's getting ready for dinner. Do you still have that meatball soup?" Marco asked.

"No." Sofia chuckled and shook her head. "One of the camera guys that I work with came to visit me today. He's a good friend of mine, and he hasn't seen me in a while because I haven't been doing any filming lately. So when he came by, I offered him some soup and other things for lunch. He loved it and finished it all."

"Oh, I understand! You offer other men soup too?" Marco said it sarcastically. "How many men come to your house to eat your soup? But that's fine. I wanted to come and see you, but if you don't have any soup, then I'll go home instead and have some of the pierogis you gave me the other day."

Sofia was very annoyed by Marco's comment about the soup and men. "Yes, when I have guests I offer them my hospitality and kindness, including food, especially if they're my good friends. That's how I was raised. Can I ask you a question, Marco? Did you really want to see me today, or did you just want to come to have soup?" Sofia was getting very upset.

"Both."

"Well, unfortunately, I don't have it! Go and enjoy dinner with your friends. I have to go now. I've got a lot to do. Good night." Sofia hung up the phone. She was so mad at him.

In a few seconds, Marco called her back, but Sofia didn't answer the phone. Marco knew the comment that he had made about other men and her soup had upset Sofia. He texted her because he knew she wouldn't answer his call.

Marco texted, "Objectively, life is shorter for me than you. What is left for me to do is to live lightly, laugh, love, be kind, and have fun. If any one of these ingredients is missing, the recipe is incomplete, and the taste of life sours. My humor is not meant to offend you. However, I see that it does. It's a shame, and I apologize."

Sofia replied, "Unfortunately, my understanding of your humor is lacking in precision. I don't do well with innuendo or veiled humor. To make the recipe complete for us, we need to have concise communication in all aspects of life. I love to laugh as long as I understand the joke, but I did not feel that way after our conversation. Thanks for your apology."

Marco texted back, "Dear Sofia, You understood my reference, and it annoyed you. The joke about men coming to eat your soup was just that. I was planning to come see you without the soup, of course. However, I could not reach you. Moving forward, I wish you a positive outcome with the doctor tomorrow. Good night."

Sofia read Marco's text but didn't reply. She put her phone down and was very sad. She tried to hold back her tears, but they dropped from her eyes while she sat on her couch, holding the script and reading her lines.

CASTING ROOM—DAY

There were several women in the room, including Sofia, sitting and waiting to audition. Sofia was breathing deeply and secretly checking her catheter bag to make sure it didn't get filled up. She was wearing a beautiful long dress to hide it, but she looked very sad and was quite nervous. An interior door opened, and the casting director came out and called Sofia's name: "Next is Sofia Novak…"

Sofia got up. "Hi."

"Hi, Sofia. Come with me," the casting director said.

In the audition room, there were two people sitting and one camera guy standing. Sofia entered the room and smiled at everyone; she completely changed her attitude. She was very confident and looked secure. She stood with very beautiful posture, and it was very easy to see that she'd been a dancer. The casting director started asking her questions.

"Are you a dancer?"

"Yes, I used to dance," Sofia responded with a smile.

"Where are you originally from?"

"From Poland."

"What kind of dance did you perform?" the casting director asked.

"Polish folk dancing," Sofia responded. She was hoping that they wouldn't ask her to perform anything because her catheter bag would drop on the floor. It was already getting filled up. She just wanted to audition and leave. She kept looking down and checking her dress while she was talking.

"That's great! OK, whenever you're ready you can start."

Sofia felt relieved and started her audition. She was playing a dance teacher in her studio where she was teaching a couple how to dance. Sofia began her lines: "And one, two, three, four…one, two, three, four…"

OUTSIDE THE CASTING DIRECTOR'S OFFICE—DAY

Sofia was leaving the audition room and looked very uncomfortable. Her catheter was bothering her, and her positive mood had dissipated. She was very close to a park, so she decided to walk a little bit before going home. She saw a beautiful tree in front of her and decided to sit down underneath it. For a minute she closed her eyes. Then she heard her phone ringing. She took out her phone and saw that Marco was calling her. She answered. "Hi." Sofia sounded sad.

"Hummingbird, how are you? Did they remove the catheter?"

"No, they didn't. And they told me that I still need to have it for another two weeks. The doctor said that it usually takes from three to five weeks to be able to go to the bathroom by yourself. I'm devastated, and I just had an audition a few minutes ago. I had to come here with my catheter, and I feel awful."

"Oh, God. Sofia, I am so sorry to hear all that." Marco felt Sofia's sadness and was embarrassed by what he had said to her the day before.

"Marco, it's bad enough that I have this damn catheter, but I'm really upset by the way you treated me on the phone yesterday. I thought you would come and see me. It was the Fourth of July…and the only thing you wanted was my soup!"

"Sofia, listen, I wanted to come. I called you back right after our conversation, but you didn't answer the phone, so that's why I texted you. But you didn't want to talk or text because you were upset. Of course I wanted to see *you*. I was just *joking* about the soup."

Sofia got really emotional.

"If you wanted to see me, then you would have come—you knew I was home by myself. Let me tell you this: when you take me out to those fancy restaurants for dinner, it's not that I want to go to those places to eat. Please don't get me wrong. I appreciate going out, and I'm grateful that you want to take me. But you know that I don't eat anything that late in the evening, and I'm not desperate to go to the hottest restaurants in town. For me, the most important thing is that when we go to those places, I just want to be with *you* and spend time with *you*. That's what I want. Because I *care about you*, and I'm *happy with you, Marco*. The rest is secondary." Sofia reached an emotional peak and was ready to burst into tears, but she was trying so hard to hold herself back. Her voice was a little shaky. "But what you said yesterday showed me that you just wanted to come and see me only if I had *soup* for you. That hurt me…How would you feel if you were in my situation? And now you're saying that you wanted to come? If you did, you didn't need my invitation, you would have come. *But you didn't, did you?*" Sofia paused. She felt her catheter bag filling up, and she was starting to feel uncomfortable. "Marco, I have to go. I can't talk any longer."

Marco was speechless. He was touched and moved by Sofia's words and felt ashamed. "OK, go, go, and I'll call you later."

Sofia hung up the phone and checked her catheter. She realized that she was bleeding because the catheter bag's contents were red. She wanted to get up, but she had severe pain in her stomach. The pain increased dramatically, and she couldn't even move. She didn't know what to do and was very scared. She picked up her phone, hardly able to breathe, and dialed 911. She tried to scream, "Help, help!" but she couldn't even scream because the pain was overwhelming.

COMMUNITY GENERAL HOSPITAL, EMERGENCY ROOM—DAY

Marco was walking with Sofia outside of the emergency room. His car was in front of the door. He opened the car door for her and helped her get into the car. Then he closed the door and walked around to the driver's side.

He opened the door, sat down, and started driving—in silence.

Two Weeks Later

COMMUNITY GENERAL HOSPITAL, EXAM ROOM—MORNING

Finally, after a month of having a catheter, Sofia was getting it removed. The nurse was withdrawing the catheter and teaching Sofia how to catheterize herself because she still couldn't pee on her own.

"You have to learn how to catheterize yourself because you can't keep this catheter in any longer. If you do, you'll get more infections, and the doctor doesn't want you to get used to relying on the catheter. And you really should be able to pee by now anyway. So I think if you learn how to catheterize yourself, it will be helpful, and you might pee on your own sooner rather than later." The nurse tried to convince Sofia to learn how to catheterize herself.

Sofia looked very frustrated and scared. She said, "I understand, but when you put the catheter in, it was so painful. I can't even imagine putting it in by myself. I can't do this."

The nurse was very nice and kept trying to explain that self-catheterizing was not as painful as a regular catheter. "The catheter that you have now is much thicker than the one that you'll be using on your own. It's very thin and much easier to use and insert. I'll show it to you, and you can just try it once. If you can't do it, then we can talk to your doctor. OK?"

Finally, the nurse persuaded Sofia to try it. She had everything ready: she put a big mirror in front of Sofia and showed her the process. Then Sofia picked up a thin catheter, but she was very scared and shaking. "God, help me," she said. She paused a little bit, and then put the catheter straight into her bladder with confidence and ease. "It worked…Oh my God…I did it! It's not that hard or painful. Oh, thank you…thank you." Sofia's eyes were full of happy tears. She wanted to scream with joy, and she was finally relieved.

The nurse was also happy for Sofia. "I told you…It's not that hard! But I think you're very, very good." The nurse looked impressed because she hadn't been expecting this from Sofia. "A lot of people have a hard time learning this, and some can never do it. But you, especially on your first try, did an excellent job. You don't need to try it again. You can do it very easily at home.

Just make sure that every three to four hours you catheterize yourself, and don't ever go longer than five hours. If you feel like you need to go in two hours, that's fine as long as you don't wait too long."

"OK, I'll do everything. Thanks so much…I feel better now." Sofia felt free, and she was grateful and more relaxed.

SOFIA'S APARTMENT—SAME DAY

Sofia opened the house door and rushed in quickly. She immediately opened her bag, got her little catheter out, dropped her bag on the floor, and ran straight to the bathroom. She was holding the catheter in her hand, but before she even opened it, she decided to sit down on the toilet first. She held her breath and suddenly peed by herself without any hesitation. Her eyes were getting big, and she started screaming! She was flushed and full of emotions.

"*I can pee. I can peeeeeeeeeeeeee…Oh my God…I can pee*! I can't believe this…*Thank you, God*…and the *universe*! *Thank you, thank you, thank you!*" Sofia was screaming so loudly and crying and laughing at the same time. It was an incredible scene of jubilation. She was exhilarated that she had finally peed on her own again, and she was hugging and kissing herself while sitting on the toilet.

Three Weeks Later

MARCO'S CAR—MORNING

It was early in the morning. Marco and Sofia were out in his Ferrari. While Marco was driving, Sofia was trying to drink her coffee, but Marco was driving very fast, and the movement of the car caused her to spill a little coffee on her clothes. Sofia felt uncomfortable because she needed to constantly hold her coffee cup since there was no cup holder in the car. She was trying to eat a chocolate croissant at the same time, but Marco stopped her.

"Are you going to eat that croissant in here?"

"Yes, do you want some?"

"No, I don't, and we'll be at the hotel soon, so we can eat there."

Sofia shook her head and smiled. "All right, I can wait. I know you don't want me to make your car messy. Even if I eat the croissant, I wouldn't make a mess, but don't worry, I'll wait."

Sofia was sipping her coffee and again spilled a little bit of it on her clothes. Marco kept glancing over at Sofia because he was obsessed with his car and didn't want her to spill coffee on the seat. Sofia saw him looking over at her and knew how much he loved his car. "I'm being careful, don't worry."

"Do you like my car?" Marco asked and quickly looked at Sofia.

"Actually, I don't." Sofia was always very uncomfortable in his car, and she responded quickly and honestly.

Marco was a little offended. "Oh, really? You don't? You have *no idea* how hard I worked in my life to be able to buy this car. This is my dream."

"Marco, I understand what you're saying. But you asked me a question, and I gave you my honest and sincere answer. If I had enough money to be able to buy this car, I wouldn't because this isn't my type of car. I'm not comfortable in it. But I *do know* the value of a *Ferrari*, and I know what a prestigious, classy, and luxurious car it is. It's beautiful and a great car for you, and I'm glad that you have it because it suits you. But it's just not my style." Then with a smile Sofia said, "I like big cars."

Marco responded sarcastically, "OK. Hopefully, your next boyfriend will have a truck!"

"Thank you. I hope so too!" Sofia was a bit annoyed, but she knew that Marco was being silly, so she tried to take it easy on him and still be clear. "Marco, would you be happier if I said what you wanted to hear, or do you really want my truthful opinion?"

Marco smiled at Sofia and changed his attitude. "You're right. I appreciate your sincerity and honesty."

SUNSET ROCK RESORT, LAGUNA BEACH, CALIFORNIA—DAY

They entered the Sunset Rock Resort grounds and stopped the car in front of the entrance. The valets opened the car doors to let Sofia and Marco out of the car. The valets also took their luggage out, and Marco and Sofia walked together into the hotel lobby.

Sofia was standing in the lobby and admiring the outstanding view of Laguna Beach. She looked happy and relaxed. Marco finished checking in and walked over to Sofia. He approached her from behind and wrapped his arms around her. "Do you like the view?"

"I love it! This is so beautiful. I'm so happy to be here with you."

"I'm happy too!" Marco kissed Sofia on her neck. Sofia turned and hugged Marco. Then they looked at each other, and Marco quickly touched his lips and remembered that he had a small blister on his lip.

"I told you before. Once in a while, I get this small blister on my lip, especially when I'm out in the sun. It only happens maybe once a year or even every two years. But don't worry. I've had it my whole life, and it isn't contagious." Even though Marco was the one giving the explanation, he still felt uncomfortable about having it.

Sofia wasn't concerned about Marco's blister at all. She touched his lips with her hand and kissed him right away to make him feel comfortable.

"I get one or two pimples on my face once in a while too. Don't worry about it. It's not even that noticeable," Sofia said lovingly.

"OK. Let's go upstairs. We can change and go to the beach."

"Sounds great," Sofia responded. Marco took Sofia's hand, and they walked to the elevator.

LAGUNA BEACH—DAY

Marco and Sofia swam together; played in the waves, jumping and diving; and laughed a lot. Sofia loved swimming, and both she and Marco were good swimmers. After they were done with swimming, they climbed up some huge, very scary rocks, but they both bravely made it to the top where they sat together to watch the beautiful ocean waves.

Late in the afternoon, Marco and Sofia went to a store where Marco bought a bathing suit for Sofia and a few other things. Then soon after, they were sitting in the lobby together, relaxing and listening to the piano player and enjoying some champagne. The pianist suddenly started to play a waltz, and Marco got up, took Sofia's hands, and invited her to dance. They danced together beautifully. Marco remembered all the steps that Sofia had taught him, and they both appreciated the moment. At the end of the dance, a few people in the lobby clapped and smiled at them.

SUNSET ROCK RESORT, HOTEL ROOM, BATHROOM—EVENING

Marco was in the bathroom standing in front of the mirror and holding a needle. He proceeded to poke the blister on his lip, and his lip started bleeding. Sofia called to him from the bedroom. "Marco…Marco…" Sofia first knocked on the bathroom door and then opened it. She saw that Marco was bleeding from his lip. There was blood in the sink and on his shirt. "What did you do?" Sofia looked very concerned. "Oh no, Marco."

"I'm fine, don't worry. I hate when I get this blister. I wanna get rid of it," Marco said calmly.

"You shouldn't have done it. Isn't it painful?"

"Not really…I'm fine. I'll be ready in a few minutes. You should get ready, too, because we're having dinner at seven." While Marco was talking, he was also cleaning up, washing his hands and rinsing his face.

"OK," Sofia said, and she walked out of the bathroom.

SUNSET ROCK RESORT, RESTAURANT—EVENING

Marco and Sofia were dressed up stylishly but appropriately for the beach and were enjoying dinner on the restaurant's patio. It was a gorgeous evening, and there was an outstanding view of the beach, the ocean, and the full moon. Sofia picked up her glass and made a toast.

"Marco, I am having the most beautiful time ever with you, and I want to thank you for making this trip so unforgettable." She paused a little bit before saying, "I love you."

"Oh, my sweet hummingbird!" Marco was so happy to hear that. His eyes were sparkling like the stars, and he was so thrilled to hear Sofia's sweet and loving words. "You are so very special to me!"

Marco leaned toward Sofia, and they kissed.

After dinner, they walked together on the beach late into the evening, holding hands and looking at the moon. They were playful, cheerful, and upbeat while enjoying their amazing evening. Then abruptly, Marco stopped walking, pulled Sofia close to him, hugged her tightly, and kissed her passionately.

Four Days Later

SOFIA'S APARTMENT—DAY

Sofia opened her apartment door and was holding her travel bag. She had just come back from her trip with Marco. She dropped her bag in the hallway and heard her phone ring. She got her phone out from her purse and saw that Nick was calling.

"Hi, honey. How are you?"

"I miss you, Mommy. I can't wait to see you tomorrow."

"Me too! I can't wait either. How's Jessie?"

"She's fine. Mom, is Maddie coming with you?" Nick loved Maddie, and he always enjoyed her company.

"Yes, Maddie is coming. But she won't be leaving 'til late afternoon tomorrow, so we'll be driving separately. She's looking forward to seeing everyone."

"Wow, that's great! After you come tomorrow, can we stay a few more days? My school doesn't start 'til next week, so we still have time, and I don't want to go back right away." Nick couldn't wait to hear his mom's response.

"Absolutely, we can. Maddie and I already decided to stay until Saturday," Sofia responded with a smile.

"Yayyyyyy! Thank you, Mommy!" Nick was thrilled that he could stay one more week at Jessie's.

"You're really having a great time there, huh?"

"I'm having an awesome time. I want to go back with you, but I want to stay here as long as we can."

"That's wonderful. I'm happy that you're enjoying your summer. OK, honey, say hi to Jessie, and I'll see you tomorrow. I love you!"

"Love you too, Mom!"

They both hung up the phone.

SOFIA'S APARTMENT, BEDROOM—MORNING

It was 7:00 a.m. Sofia was coming out of the bathroom and had some personal belongings in her hands: a small cosmetic bag, lotion, shampoo, etc. She was dressed and getting ready for her drive to Northern California. Her travel bag was packed, but she didn't look well. She felt very uncomfortable because something was bothering her again—sort of like when she had the catheter. She walked back and forth very uncomfortably and felt very itchy. Finally, she picked up her purse only and left the house without her travel bag. It was still in the hallway.

COMMUNITY GENERAL HOSPITAL, URGENT CARE EXAM ROOM—DAY

Sofia was lying down on the exam table, and the doctor was doing a gynecology exam. The female doctor finished her inspection and looked up at Sofia, who was in obvious pain.

"You have genital herpes. The herpes virus causes these types of blisters, and unfortunately, you have four of them. This is going to be very painful, but I have to cut the blisters to drain them."

Sofia screamed loudly while the doctor cut the blisters. She was in pain, but at the same time, she looked totally bewildered and didn't understand what the doctor was saying.

"Oh my God—what do I have? What do you mean I have the herpes virus?" Sofia was in severe pain and was totally confused because she didn't know anything about the herpes virus. She could barely speak. "Can you please explain it to me? What does that mean?"

"What you have is genital herpes caused by the herpes virus, which is permanent. It's not curable, but it's manageable. When you have an outbreak like you have now, the blisters can be very painful."

"That's impossible. I've never had any virus. I am one hundred percent healthy. I don't understand. How did I get this?" Sofia sounded utterly lost.

"You could have contracted it from your partner. Did your partner have any blisters or sores anywhere while having sexual contact with you?"

The doctor finished her procedure, took her gloves off, and washed her hands. She was writing something on the computer while talking to Sofia. Sofia's eyes started to get big when she recalled that Marco had had a blister on his lip when they were in Laguna Beach. In a shocked and confused voice, she said, "Yes, he had a blister on his lip, but I didn't know it was the herpes virus. I thought it was just a blister, like a pimple. And then he burst it with a needle, and it was bleeding. *Oh noooo…*"

The doctor was shaking her head. She felt sorry for Sofia because of the situation, but she didn't want to say anything more. "Unfortunately, that blister was herpes. He shouldn't have burst it because he exposed you to it. I'll prescribe an antiviral medication that should help you. You need to take it twice a day for seven days. I'll write everything down for you. I'm so sorry that you're going through this."

Sofia was speechless and shocked. She didn't know what to say. She looked very disoriented but got up from the table to change.

COMMUNITY GENERAL HOSPITAL, PHARMACY—DAY

Sofia was sitting on a chair in the pharmacy waiting for her medication. She looked pale, sad, and distressed. She was holding her phone in her hand and paused for a few seconds before she started writing a text to Marco.

"Marco, I had terrible vaginal pain last night and couldn't sleep at all. This morning I decided to go and see a doctor before driving to Northern California. Unfortunately I was diagnosed with herpes. The doctor said if my partner had any sores anywhere then that would be how I contracted it because it is contagious. It's very painful, and right now I'm in the pharmacy getting an antiviral medication. Within the hour, I'll be heading north. I'll be OK—don't worry about me. Talk to you soon."

Sofia sent the text and then got up to see if her medication was ready. Suddenly she heard her name. Sofia approached the pharmacist and got instructions about the medication.

SOFIA'S CAR—SAME DAY

Sofia was driving north. Her phone rang, and it was Marco.

"Hi, Marco." Sofia sounded tired.

"Sofia, how are you? I don't know what to say. I can't believe this. I've had this blister on and off since I was maybe nineteen or twenty years old, and I've never ever infected any woman in my entire life. You know I've been with a lot of women, and I had a wife for eight years. We were intimate even when I had the blister, and she never got this from me. I would never ever have believed that this would have been contagious. Oh God, Sofia…I am so sorry. I know you're driving…I feel horrible."

"That's OK. I'm a little better now. I took the medication, and I feel weak, but I'm able to drive. I had four blisters like yours, and the doctor needed to cut them to drain them. It was very, very painful, and I was screaming…"

While Sofia was talking about her condition, Marco was hardly breathing and was struggling with his thoughts as he listened to everything that Sofia had to say.

"This is crazy! I wish you weren't driving. You should have stayed with me. I can't believe this..."

"I can't believe it either. Marco, the blister on your lip that you said comes out in the sun is the herpes virus. It's a cold sore that's very contagious, and you can't have any oral contact when you have that sore. So when you took that needle and burst open the blister on your lip, it released the virus and became highly contagious. I didn't know anything about herpes and cold sores. If I did, I would have protected myself and you too."

Marco was devastated. He was in his office at his desk, and he was broken by this horrible turn of events.

"Sofia...of course, you're right, and the doctor is absolutely right. It *is* contagious, and I am *soooo stupid*. I wasn't thinking at the time. I have *never ever* infected any woman in my life. And because I've had this blister since I was very young, I didn't think that it would be contagious, and I wouldn't have wanted to infect anyone, especially you. You know how much I care about you. I wanted to take you to Laguna Beach to show you how much you mean to me and how much I appreciate having you in my life. I never ever wanted to hurt you. If I had the tiniest thought at the moment that this blister would have been dangerous, I never would have had sex with you that night. But this was a pure mistake. I didn't think about it as a virus or something that was contagious and dangerous. *I would never ever harm you…*you know that. I am stupid. I am very stupid! I wish you weren't driving and had come to me after the doctor's appointment. I feel so terrible…I don't know what to say. *I am so sorry…*Sofia, I feel so bad…*I am so sorry!*"

"I know, Marco, I believe you. I don't blame you because I know that this was just an honest mistake on your part. I really believe that. I know that you never ever intentionally wanted to do something like this. There is no question about it. I've always trusted you, and I was never concerned about anything with you."

Marco was unhinged and shocked by hearing Sofia's calm, generous, kind, and loving words. He didn't know what to say.

"That's what's *killing* me! I know how much you trusted me, and I let you down. Everything you're saying is *killing* me. I want to die and not hear all that." Marco was so shattered that he didn't know how to handle Sofia's gracious attitude. "Sofia, please drive safe. I don't want to add to your stress, but I'm going to keep checking on you. Just know that I'm here for you, and I'm thinking of you every second."

"OK, Marco…I'll be fine. Talk to you soon."

They both hung up the phone. Marco was still sitting at his desk with his face buried in his hands, totally overwhelmed. He heard someone knocking on his office door, and in a few seconds, the door opened. It was Scott, Marco's assistant.

"Marco, can I speak with you?" Scott asked quietly.

"What is it Scott?" Marco sounded very stern.

Scott sensed Marco's emotions and attitude. He was uncertain as to whether he should speak now, but he mustered up the courage to speak.

"It's just that this...um...one of the tenants from the Atari Apartments still hasn't made his payments."

Marco was pissed off and didn't want to hear this now. "Scott...*And what*? You can't deal with him? *Fuck him*...and he will pay! I hired *you* and the *others* over there so I don't need to go through this *shit*! *Call him and say, 'Fuck you!'* And if he still doesn't pay, then scream loudly, *'Fuck you!'*" Marco yelled loudly...over and over again. "Do you get it?" There was silence for a few seconds, and then Marco said, "OK, give me his number and name."

"Yes, here it is." Scott was intimidated but quickly approached Marco and handed him the piece of paper with the name and contact information of the tenant. Marco took the paper, got his phone, and dialed the number. The tenant, Tom Burke picked up the phone.

"Hello?"

"Hi…is this Mr. Burke?" Marco was very angry.

"Yes, that's me."

"This is Marco Morelli, the president of Prestigious Properties." Marco was very loud and almost yelling. "You have *one hour* to make a direct payment to Prestigious Properties, Inc. If you don't make this payment, I will send the security team. They will lock the gates and be instructed not to let you into your apartment building until you make your *fucking* payment. *Is that clear?*" Marco was so loud that Scott was looking at him alarmingly.

"Yes…I will send the check right now. No problem, Mr. Morelli." The tenant sounded very intimidated, and his voice was very quiet.

Marco hung up the phone and looked very angrily at Scott. Scott looked frightened and just wanted to disappear. "He will send the check right now. Next time, I don't want to deal with this kind of *fucking shit*! Do you understand me? Handle it by yourself!"

"Yes, Boss," Scott replied. He quickly walked out of Marco's office.

JESSIE'S HOUSE—LATE AFTERNOON

Sofia parked her car in the driveway and was getting out of it when Nick suddenly opened the front door of the house and ran to his mom. They hugged each other.

"Hi, honey! Oh, I missed you sooooo much! Look how much you've grown...unbelievable! My big boy...I love you!"

Nick was so happy to see his mom. He grabbed the travel bag from her. "Let me help you, Mom. I missed you too. Is Maddie gonna be here soon?"

"Yes, she'll be here in about an hour."

They both went into the house.

Jessie greeted Sofia and was so happy to see her. Sofia hugged and kissed Jessie.

"Hi, sweetheart! I've missed you. Welcome home!"

They all headed to the kitchen. The dining table was set for four, and Jessie had everything prepared for Sofia and Maddie. Even though she was in a wheelchair, Jessie was a miracle woman. She did everything by herself: cooked, cleaned, took care of her dog. And for the entire summer, she had taken care of Nick. She was always busy and cheerful!

JESSIE'S HOUSE, DINING ROOM—EVENING

Jessie, Sofia, Maddie, and Nick were sitting at the dining table and enjoying dinner together, talking, laughing, and drinking wine. Everyone seemed very happy. Sofia tried to focus on them and not on her problems. Sofia heard her phone beep and saw that she had received a text from Marco. Sofia apologized to everyone at the table. "Please excuse me for a minute. I have to take this."

"Is everything OK, honey?" Jessie asked.

"Yes, everything's fine," Sofia responded and walked out of the dining room. She went to her bedroom and called Marco.

"Sofia, how are you? I'm thinking of you, and I'm going crazy. I wish you were here next to me." Marco sounded a little scared, concerned, and a bit different.

"I'm OK. Please don't worry about me. I'm having dinner with Jessie, Nick, and Maddie. I can't talk right now."

"Please make sure that nobody knows about this. It's our secret, and I'll make sure that you're fine. I'm here for you. How's everyone? How's Nick doing?" Marco was very stressed about the situation and didn't know how to lead the conversation.

"Everyone is fine," she said with a smile. "Nick looks great—he's grown so much. I'm happy that I'm here right now. I needed this." Sofia sensed Marco's emotions. "Marco, please...everything will be fine. I want you to be strong because that'll make me feel better and stronger. OK?" Regardless of what Sofia was going through, she was still very sweet and supportive of Marco.

"Did you take your medication?"

"I did, this morning when I got it from the pharmacy. It's a very strong medication and makes me really nauseous, but I'll take it again after dinner and before I go to bed."

Sofia was sitting on her bed while she was talking, and Marco was on the couch in his house. His head was down, and he was covering his face with his hands. He remained quiet for a few seconds, then looked up, breathing very heavily. With a firm voice he said, "Sofia... um...*I will pay you!*" Then Marco was quiet.

"What do you mean you will pay me? Pay me for what? For what happened to me? You think I want your money? You think I'm with you for your *money*? Marco, is that what you're thinking?" There was a little silence. Sofia was completely confused and didn't understand what Marco meant about paying her. In a few seconds, she got very emotional. Her voice was shaking, and she was getting angry about what Marco had said. "*I want nothing from you.* I will never ever take any penny from you. Do you hear me? I am with you because *I love you!*" Sofia's voice was shaky; she paused. "I have to go now… I don't want to talk about this anymore." Sofia got up from her bed and was about to hang up.

"*No…wait!* Sofia…Sofia, stop it! Listen to me. I'm not saying that I'll *pay you money.*" Marco knew that he had made a mistake by saying that. "I just meant that I'll pay for your medication or anything you need for your health. That's what I meant. Please don't go…wait…I would never say something like that. Please, I'm sorry if you understood it differently, but I'm here for you, and I care about you so much, and I'm very angry at myself. I'm so upset about this situation, and I don't know how to fix it. And I know that I can't fix it, and that's killing me." He paused again. "*Please forgive me…I'm sorry, I am very, very sorry.*" Marco was distraught and frightened.

"Marco, there is nothing to forgive because *I don't blame you* for this. I told you already, and I'll repeat myself again. This was just a mistake, and that's it. We all make mistakes, and I know it wasn't intentional. I believe one million percent that you never ever wanted to hurt me. I'll be fine, I promise. And right now I don't need anything, but thanks for your offer. I'm very tired and overwhelmed, and I have to go now. I'll talk to you tomorrow."

"Of course. Go and please eat well before you take your medication. Have a good night, my hummingbird."

"I will. Good night, Marco." Sofia sounded exhausted.

They both hung up the phone. Marco was still sitting on the couch, looking shocked, broken, and depressed. He started sobbing, then looked up and said, *"Forgive me, God, please forgive me."*

JESSIE'S HOUSE, BATHROOM—EVENING

Sofia was in the bathroom, getting her medication out from her cosmetic bag. She opened it and took one pill. She heard Jessie's voice in the hallway.

"Sof, honey, where are you?"

Sofia quickly opened the bathroom door and stepped out. She left everything on the bathroom counter and closed the door. Jessie was just outside the bathroom.

"I'm here, Jess."

"Is everything OK with you?" Jessie asked.

"Yes, I'm just putting some of my things in the bathroom. I'm sorry for leaving you guys in the dining room. I'm coming."

"Honey, can you go out into the garage and get the dessert from the freezer? I got your favorite cheesecake."

"Wow, you are the best, Jessie—I love it! I'll get it right now." Sofia headed down the hallway and opened the laundry room door that led to the garage.

"Oh, honey, I forgot to take out bath towels for you and Maddie," Jessie said, but then she realized that Sofia was already out in the garage and could not hear her. So Jessie decided to do it by herself. "No worries, I'll do it," she said to herself.

While Sofia was out in the garage getting the dessert from the freezer, Jessie went into Sofia's bathroom to take out some bath towels. She opened the cabinet, got the towels out, and put them on the counter where she noticed a little bottle of medication. She picked it up and read the name of the medication. She knew what it was for and put it back quickly. She came out of the bathroom and paused a little bit in the hallway because her mind was racing. She knew that Sofia was going through something major, and she was hiding it. "Shit…" she said quietly so no one heard.

JESSIE'S HOUSE, KITCHEN—NIGHT

After dinner it was already late. Jessie, Sofia, and Maddie were cleaning up together, and everyone was doing different things. Sofia was washing dishes. Maddie was almost done putting things away, and she was ready to go to bed. Maddie smiled and hugged Jessie. "Jessie, thank you so much for the delicious dinner. I am so full and ready for bed. Good night, Sofia. See you both tomorrow."

"Good night, Maddie. Thanks for your help." Sofia finished washing the dishes and was drying her hands. Maddie walked out of the kitchen. Sofia looked very tired, and she touched her stomach. She was starting to feel a little nauseous, and she was looking for some tea. Jessie noticed that Sofia looked a little uncomfortable.

"Are you OK, honey?"

"Yes, I'm just looking for…do you have ginger tea? I have my period, and I feel a little nauseous."

"I do. Open the cabinet on the right—it must be there. Sweetheart, I have to tell you something."

"Of course, what is it?" Sofia had started preparing her ginger tea.

Jessie stopped folding the kitchen towels and looked at Sofia and said, "When you went out into the garage earlier to get the dessert, I went into your bathroom to get some towels out for you and Maddie, and I saw the antiviral medication on the counter. I know what it's for, honey. Do you want to talk to me about it?"

Sofia's face changed instantly, and she felt bad that Jessie had found out about it. She didn't want Jess to know because she would start worrying about her, and it would make her stressed. "Oh no…you saw it?" Sofia did not know how to start the conversation. "OK, so, in a nutshell, Marco had a blister on his lip when we went to Laguna Beach last week. I didn't know what it was…no clue. He told me that it wasn't contagious, but unfortunately, it was, and as a result I contracted genital herpes from him. I found out about it this morning because I went to urgent care before I drove here."

In an upset voice, Jessie said, "*Shit*…sorry for my French…but that's how I feel right now. Did Marco ever tell you that he has the herpes virus?"

"No," Sofia responded with sadness in her voice. "The only thing he mentioned a while back was that he has this blister that comes out on his lip once a year or every two years when he's out in the sun. Then he said he's had it since he was nineteen or twenty years old. And even on the day when we were together in Laguna Beach, he said, 'Don't worry, this isn't *contagious*.' So I wasn't concerned at all because I thought it was just a *pimple* on his lip. I even felt like, who cares? That's fine—I have a couple of pimples on my face that come out once in a while. And then he burst it open with a needle in the bathroom." Sofia's face changed when she recalled that moment. "He said, 'This way, it'll go away soon.' I had *no clue* about the herpes virus, and I trusted Marco so much. I was absolutely sure that it was nothing." Sofia sipped her tea while Jessie listened to her intently. "I'm still very confused…I don't know what I have, although *I do*…I do…" she said quietly with a sigh. "But I know one thing for sure, and that is that this is very painful." Sofia went to the table and sat down…Everything had finally hit her.

Jessie was getting very angry. "*That fucking bastard*! I'm sorry, honey…you know I don't speak like this in this house, but I am *very, very angry at him*! If he's had this blister since he was nineteen and now he's fifty-four, right, then he *knows* that this is herpes and that *it is* contagious! He's absolutely *a fucking liar*! And when he burst it with a needle and exposed it, then had sex with you, he infected you with it. He's a *selfish and egotistical man*! He knows that this is *contagious*. You are too naive, honey. I feel horrible that you didn't know about it and he didn't have enough integrity, class, morality, or respect for you to protect you from this." Jessie's anger reached its peak, and her voice was very deep, angry, and powerful. "If he really cared about you, he should have told you what he had without question!"

Sofia got emotional. "Please, Jessie, this is *enough*! I've had enough! I'm so sick and tired of the whole thing. I don't want to hear this about him. Marco would *never ever want to hurt me*—I trust him on that. He just made a *bad mistake*. It was just an honest mistake. That's it!" Sofia got up, picked up her teacup, and put the cup in the dishwasher. She looked awful—very pale and sick—and was ready to go to bed. "Jessie, I'm sorry but I need to go to bed. I don't feel well. This medication makes me sick, and I feel like I want to throw up. I'm just exhausted from everything." Sofia had no energy at all; she was overwhelmed. "Thank you so much for the delicious dinner."

"You're welcome, honey. Go. I'm so sorry for what you're going through. Try to get some rest, and if you need anything, I'm here for you." Jessie was very upset about everything.

"Good night, Jessie." Sofia walked out of the kitchen.

JESSIE'S HOUSE, SOFIA'S BEDROOM—MORNING

It was 8:00 a.m., and Sofia's cell phone was ringing. She woke up quickly and grabbed her phone but was still quite groggy and looked sick.

"Hello?" Her voice lacked energy.

A woman said, "Hi, is this Sofia Novak?"

"Yes…" Sofia sounded concerned.

"I'm calling from Dr. Loo's office. We received your lab results, and you have a bacterial infection that was caused by the open sores. You need to go to the nearest pharmacy and fill the antibiotic prescription that your doctor gave you, and you need to take it for five days. The pharmacist will give you the details on how to take it."

Sofia was not even fully awake yet, but she was still stunned by the news. She responded to the lady on the phone, saying, "This is *crazy*! I have another infection? Oh nooo…"

"I'm sorry for that, but if you have any questions or concerns about anything, please give us a call anytime." The lady over the phone sounded very formal.

"Thank you," Sofia said without any emotion or energy.

"You're welcome. Goodbye."

Sofia was sitting on her bed with a blank expression, emotionless and in shock. She was so still and was breathing quietly. After a little pause, she looked at her phone and noticed that Marco had texted her several times: at midnight, 2:00 a.m., 6:00 a.m., and 7:00 a.m. She didn't feel up to reading all the messages right then, but she scrolled down to the last message that said, "Call me when you wake up before you take your pill." Sofia put her phone away and got up from her bed. She left the room in her pj's.

JESSIE'S HOUSE, KITCHEN—MORNING

Maddie and Nick were getting ready to go swimming outside and enjoy the day. They were very animated and excited and were joking and laughing. They both were wearing their bathing suits and getting some drinks. Jessie was in the kitchen preparing breakfast for Sofia and herself. Sofia entered the kitchen looking pale and tired, but she tried to smile and act like nothing was happening. Nick ran right to Sofia and hugged his mom.

"Good morning, sweetheart!" Sofia hugged Nick back. "Did you sleep well?" Sofia asked.

"Yes, I did. Right now Maddie and I are going out to swim, and then Billy is coming, and we're going to the movies together at four o'clock. Billy's dad is taking us." Billy had been Nick's best friend since the first grade.

"Wow, you really planned your day well—first with Maddie and then with your best friend. Sounds exciting!" With a smile Sofia looked at Maddie. "Maddie, he's keeping you busy!"

Maddie was grinning. "Absolutely. Nick and I are gonna be racing today!" Maddie laughed.

Nick ran out into the backyard with his towel and his drink and then yelled to Maddie, "Maddie, are you coming?"

"Yes, I'll be there in a minute." Maddie was concerned about Sofia's appearance. "Sofia, you look tired and pasty. Are you OK?" Sofia was making her coffee, and Jessie was putting banana bread and some jam on the table. She knew that Sofia loved all kinds of jams.

"I'm OK…um…my period just started this morning, and you know I feel terrible the first couple of days." This was another unfortunate complication that she didn't need right now.

"Oh, I know. I'm sorry. I feel the same in the beginning. All right then. I'll go outside with Nick for a little while. See you later."

In unison, Jessie and Sofia said, "Have fun."

Jessie was also very concerned; she was worried about Sofia. "How are you feeling, honey?"

"Not well," Sofia replied with mixed emotions. "This morning a nurse from my doctor's office called me. She said that I also have a bacterial infection that was caused by the open sores and I need to get another antibiotic from the pharmacy. I'll go and pick it up after breakfast.

I feel so sick now, but I need to eat. I couldn't sleep all night because it's *sooo* itchy and painful."

Jessie had already put everything on the table, and they both were sitting down to eat their breakfast. Jessie grabbed her coffee cup and looked at Sofia. She was stunned by what Sofia had just told her.

"What? Oh no…sweetheart, I am so sorry. What you're going through is *crazy*! I can't believe you have a bacterial infection too. Jesus, this summer has been just unbelievable for you. It's too much!" Jessie was getting really angry. "I just want to *kill that man*! If this happened to me, I would have shot him for sure…that *bastard*!"

"Please, Jessie, he is devastated. He already wants to die knowing what I'm going through," Sofia said in a soft and caring voice.

Jessie's anger was elevating. "Let him *die*…Serves him right!"

"*Don't* say that. I love him, and I know that Marco cares about me. He never wanted this to happen to me. This situation is killing him."

Jessie shook her head with anger. Then she said sarcastically, "Yeah, right. He really showed how much he cared when he had sex with you with his exposed blister. And he told you that he takes medication for that blister, which means he knew what he had but he withheld that from you. That shows what a selfish and egotistical bastard he is. I know you don't want to hear that, but it's the truth, and you're too gracious! He's a lucky man that this happened to you and not to any other woman."

At that moment, Sofia's cell phone rang. She looked at it and saw that it was Marco, but she didn't answer it. Then she started getting texts from him.

Sofia texted him back: "I can't talk now. I'm having breakfast and will call you soon."

"Hummingbird, please eat well and focus on being a really good actor this morning. Make it an *Academy Award performance*, and come back to LA. Let's make sure that no one knows about anything. Call me. Please call me as soon as you can."

Then Marco sent another text: "Please tell me, is your acting holding up?"

Sofia texted back: "I will call you as soon as I can."

Jessie was eating her avocado and tomato toast and drinking her coffee, but she looked angry.

Sofia looked overwhelmed, and with mixed emotions, she said, "He's worried about me. He keeps calling and texting and checking on me and asking me not to tell anyone about this. He's really worried about that. I wasn't planning to tell anyone anything. This was our secret, and it's very personal. But now you know, and I have to tell him that you found out about it. He's terrified and totally unraveled. I can't even read all his texts. He's going crazy."

"Oh, really? Now he's emotional and is worried about you? I know why he's so emotional and what he's worried about…and why he doesn't want you to tell anyone anything," Jessie said sarcastically.

Sofia was confused. She was looking at Jessie, not understanding what she was talking about.

Jessie took another bite of her toast.

"What do you mean? What is he worried about? I don't understand," Sofia responded.

Jessie put her coffee cup on the table, stopped eating, and then in a serious, solid, and angry voice said, "OK—let me tell you this. If this happened to me, I would have shot him. I told you that earlier. A certain percentage of women would have done the same. But some women would have destroyed him differently by suing him and getting as much money as possible from him. That would serve him right because he's an egotistical liar sitting on his pedestal, and what he did is immoral, unethical, and illegal. Don't forget that he is a very rich and successful man. He would pay anything—any amount—not to ruin his reputation and career. That's what he cares about the most! So these women would have fucked him over financially and would have walked away from him forever, no question about it! Sorry for my language…"

Jessie's voice kept rising up with emotions and rage. "There is only one person on this planet that would have accepted *this* so lovingly and graciously, and that's you, honey...and I don't know how you're doing it. *This is killing me!* And now you're worried about him? Let him die, let him break down, and let him go crazy! Who cares?"

"*I care*," Sofia replied in a serious, firm, and low tone. "We all make mistakes, and I think we should be forgiven for our mistakes. We should learn from them and move on. I know Marco made a terrible mistake, and he suffers from that. I can feel his devastation and regret. But I want to move on and continue this relationship with him because I love him. I believe in him, and I know that he has a wonderful heart and soul. And I know that he loves me too. I've already accepted what I got from him because this is the only way I can move on and leave the past behind. I hope Marco can forgive himself and accept what happened so he can move on too. You know, our connection ever since we met is like nothing I've ever experienced before. Even with Nick's dad, I didn't have this intensity of emotion. Right from the very beginning, it was like Marco and I were destined to be together. We both instantly bonded and felt like we had known each other for years. Maybe we did in another life—who knows? This isn't just a fleeting love affair…I'm convinced that we're soul mates on this journey together."

Jessie was stunned by Sofia's love and graciousness toward Marco. "Are you *nuts*? You're a better woman than me or anyone that I know."

With a caring and soft voice, Sofia said, "Jessie, I totally understand that your anger and frustration is because you love me. But please…I'm asking you to forgive him. You know how much I love you, and I want you to support me in whatever decision I make with my life. I know Marco better than anyone, so let's not talk about him like this. Let's try to move on. I think that'll be better for all of us because I'm not feeling well, and I need to get over the side effects of this medication, get rid of the pain, and heal myself. Right now, I just need some solitude!"

Sofia got up with her dish and coffee cup and put them in the sink. Then she grabbed her purse and phone and looked at Jessie with a little smile on her face. "I'll be back soon."

Sofia walked out of the kitchen. Jessie was speechless and looked very moved by Sofia's words.

MARCO'S HOUSE, LIVING ROOM—DAY

Marco was nervously walking back and forth in the living room of his house. He was still dressed in his work clothes but looked awful. His eyes were red, and he was visibly emotional. He went to his bedroom and sat on the bed. He was holding his cell phone and looking at the photos that he took with Sofia in Laguna Beach. He looked totally destroyed. A few seconds later, he checked his texts to see if Sofia had texted anything. He was waiting to hear from her, but he was so impatient that he called her again. Sofia was driving but picked up the call on her headset.

"Hi, Marco." Sofia's voice had only a little energy.

"Hummingbird…how are you feeling? Are you driving? I'm going insane here not being able to see you or be there with you." Marco sounded very nervous.

"The nurse called me from my doctor's office this morning. The lab result showed that I also have a bacterial infection caused by the open sores, so I have to get an antibiotic from the pharmacy. That's where I'm going now. It's bad enough that the antiviral that I'm taking makes me sick…just the thought of taking an antibiotic on top of that already makes me nauseous."

After hearing what Sofia said, Marco got up from the sofa and started moving around with anxiety.

"Fuck," he said it quietly. Then a little more forcefully, he repeated, "Fuck." Then loudly, he said, "For God's sake!" He sighed. "I am *so sorry*! Please don't let anyone know you're getting that prescription. I'll send you a driver, or I'll come and drive you and Nick back home tomorrow morning. I'll take care of your car—don't worry about it. Or I'll fly you both back to LA. Just tell me, what do you want me to do? Please leave tomorrow."

Sofia entered the pharmacy parking lot and parked right in front but stayed in the car and continued the conversation.

"Marco, I can't do that. First of all, I don't feel well, and I'd rather stay here with Jessie than go back there with Nick right now. I need to be here for a few more days. I'm exhausted, sick, and overwhelmed with everything. Jessie and Maddie are a big help, and they're taking care of me. So please give me some time to heal. I'll be fine." She paused for a moment. "There's one more thing I need to tell you. You know I wasn't planning to talk about this whole situation with anyone, but Jessie accidently saw the antiviral medication in my bathroom, and she knows what it's for. So I told her what happened."

"*Shit*. Sorry, Sofia…I feel *horrible*. I'm sure she thinks I'm a fucking…terrible man! She hates me now for sure.

That's why I didn't want anyone to know." Marco sounded so stressed and overwrought.

"Marco, I wasn't planning to tell anyone, but it happened, and I can't help it. Jessie doesn't hate you. I explained everything that happened, and she's just disappointed in you and feels terrible for me because of what I'm going through." Sofia tried to calm Marco.

"I'll call her and apologize for everything, or I can even go and see her in person."

"No, please, no. Right now, I don't think that's a good idea. Everyone needs time to get over this initial shock. Please don't worry. We're planning to leave on Saturday depending on how I feel."

"Please let me help you now to bring you and Nick back on Saturday. I'll take care of everything."

"Can we talk about that later? I appreciate it, but I need to go now and pick up my medication. I feel very weak and want to go home."

"Of course. Please go and know that I'm with you, and I promise you, my little hummingbird, you will *fly high again*. Please believe me...*higher and stronger than before!*"

"I believe you...I'm happy that I have you in my life. I'm sending you my kiss. Bye, Marco."

They both hung up the phone. Sofia got out of the car and suddenly felt very sick, like she was going to throw up. She quickly walked to the pharmacy, went inside, and ran to the bathroom. She threw up in the toilet, and after a few moments, she came out of the stall looking very pale and completely wiped out. She washed her face with cold water and looked in the mirror for a few seconds. Her eyes were red and tired.

JESSIE'S HOUSE, JESSIE'S BEDROOM—MIDNIGHT

It was 2:00 a.m., and everyone was sleeping except for Jessie. Her television was on, and faint light was shining out from underneath her closed bedroom door. Sofia was in her bed but couldn't sleep. She felt sick, and she could not find the right position to get comfortable, so she got up to get some water from the kitchen and noticed the light coming from Jessie's room. She lightly tapped on the bedroom door, opened it, and called out to Jessie

"Jessie…are you OK?" She saw that Jessie was in her bed.

"I'm fine, honey. I woke up with terrible leg cramps, so I'm just trying to stretch them a little bit. Come on in…What are you doing up?"

"I couldn't get comfortable in bed and have been tossing and turning since midnight. And this medication makes me incredibly nauseous."

"Come and sit down. I'm really worried about you."

Sofia sat down in Jessie's wheelchair, close to her bed. Even though she looked exhausted, she was trying to cheer Jessie up. Sofia was always ready to do something funny to bring some joy into life.

"Please don't worry about me…I'll be OK, eventually. I'd rather be here with you right now. OK, let me give you a leg and foot massage. Maybe it will help you a little bit."

Sofia smiled, grabbed Jessie's leg, and started giving her a massage. While she was doing it, she felt uncomfortable and very itchy from the blisters, so she started squirming around to quell the itch. Her face looked so funny that it made Jessie laugh. Although Sofia didn't do it intentionally, she always had this little comedic essence, and sometimes she did things without even knowing how funny she really was. Jessie tried to hold her laughter. "You're crazy…and so funny," Jessie said. "Oh, that feels really good…Thank you, sweetheart, for the massage. Sometimes I can't take you seriously. The way you do things makes me laugh. Although what you have isn't funny and it's killing me to watch you go through this, your facial expressions when you're trying to 'scratch your itch' are hilarious!"

They both started laughing. Sofia finished one leg and grabbed the other one to massage.

"You know what…how can I ever complain about anything? When I look at you, I think you're the strongest, bravest, toughest, and most incredible woman I've ever known in my life. All of these years that I've known you, you've never complained about your MS or anything else. I don't know how you're doing it. And you're telling me that I'm a better woman than you? I don't think so…No one is like you. I am so blessed to have you in my life," Sofia said with a loving and encouraging voice.

After a short pause, Sofia started singing Stevie Wonder's song "I Just Called to Say I Love You."

Sofia sang the first line: *I just called to say I love you.*

Jessie joined her, and they sang together.

> *I just called to say how much I care,*
> *I just called to say I love you,*
> *And I mean it from the bottom of my heart.*

They looked at each other with love, and they both smiled.

Saturday

SOFIA'S APARTMENT—EVENING

Sofia was opening her house door. She and Nick entered their apartment carrying their bags. They had just returned from Northern California. Nick took his bag and went straight to his bedroom. While Nick was on his way up the stairs, Sofia said loudly, "Nick, go and take a shower and put all of your dirty clothes in the laundry room."

"OK, Mom," Nick replied.

At that moment, Sofia's cell phone rang. She grabbed her phone from her purse. Marco was calling her.

"Hi, Marco."

"Is my hummingbird back in her nest with her boy?" Marco was driving.

"Yes, we are…we just came in."

"You sound exhausted. I just wanted to make sure that you're both OK and arrived safely. I can't wait to see you and Nick tomorrow. Did you guys eat well? Especially you?"

"Yes, we stopped on our way and had dinner."

"OK, then. Please go and rest, and I'll see you tomorrow. I missed you so much!"

"I missed you too! See you tomorrow—good night."

SOFIA'S APARTMENT—EVENING

The doorbell rang, and Nick ran to the door. He opened it, and Marco was standing there with a huge bouquet of sunflowers in a vase and two big bags of groceries. He was dressed up neatly.

"Hi, Nick, it's so good to see you. You've grown so much this summer." Marco patted Nick on his head.

"Good to see you too, Marco. Let me help you." Nick grabbed a bag and helped Marco as he came in.

"Thanks, Nick." Marco handed him a grocery bag, then entered the house.

Sofia was in the kitchen, and the table was set in the dining room. She had prepared dinner for everyone and was getting a few dishes ready to put on the table. Marco and Nick walked into the kitchen.

"Wow! Hi, Marco." Sofia and Marco hugged each other. "What a beautiful bouquet…I love sunflowers!" Sofia grabbed them from Marco's hand.

"I know you do, and yellow is also your favorite color," Marco said with a smile.

Sofia kissed Marco and put the vase on the table. She looked happy, and Marco kissed her back with the same happiness.

"I missed you so much! These groceries are for you and Nick—I want you to eat well. I got you some protein shakes, too, because you need lots of protein. I hope I got everything that you like."

"Oh, you're so thoughtful! Thank you for buying all of these goodies. I'm sure that Nick and I will love everything. You guys take these two plates and put them on the table. I'll just put these groceries in the fridge so they don't go bad. It'll only take me a minute."

Marco and Nick put a few dishes on the dining table.

"Nick, tell me what you did over the summer. Did you have fun?"

"Yes, I did. Mostly, I was hanging out with my friends, going to the movies, playing basketball, riding bikes, and playing Xbox. It was fun. But Jessie made me do math every day."

"Playing basketball is great, and I know you really love it. You're tall, and you'll grow a lot more, but you're too skinny. You need to build up your muscles. Your mom always complains that you're a very picky eater. You need to eat lots of protein to strengthen your muscles. You have to work out every single day, play basketball, and most importantly, eat well. If you want, we can make a chart to keep track of your weight and the size of your arms, quads, calves, shoulders, chest, and waist. If you want to be a successful basketball player, first you have to believe it, then work very, very hard to accomplish it!"

Sofia entered the dining room and lit the candle on the table. Then everyone sat down.

"Well, Marco—Nick and I are happy that you joined us tonight. Please help yourself…"

"I am more than grateful that I'm with you both tonight." Marco poured some drinks in everybody's glasses, and they started to enjoy their dinner.

SOFIA'S APARTMENT, KITCHEN—AFTER DINNER

Sofia and Marco were cleaning up everything in the kitchen. Marco was putting the last of the dishes away while Sofia was preparing tea. Nick was already in bed. Marco sat down at the table looking very sad and depressed. While Nick was with them, Marco tried his best not to show any emotions or frustrations. But now he was visibly shaken.

"Sofia, I am very sorry for what I did. I can never forgive myself for this…I hurt you. Please forgive me," Marco said quietly with sadness and pain.

"Marco, please, we've already talked about this. I don't need to forgive you because I don't blame you for what happened. If you want me to repeat this over and over, I can do it. You know that. *I love you*…and I want to be with you. I want to move on and forget the past. I know it hurts you, but we don't have any other choice. We can't fix this; it's permanent. I can manage it, and I can take care of myself, but I want you to be with me and help me through this."

Marco's head was hanging down, and he couldn't even look at Sofia. He was hardly breathing and felt terrible.

"I can't sleep at night thinking about this. Every day while you were gone I was thinking of you…how much I hurt you…and I was crying every single day."

Sofia put her teacup on the table and approached Marco. She embraced him and sat on his lap. Marco embraced her back and started sobbing. Sofia kissed him on his neck and his cheeks, trying to make him feel better.

"You are my sweet Marco… I love you."

Marco abruptly got up, pulling Sofia from his lap. He got even more frustrated and mad when he felt the love that Sofia had for him. He was still scared about what he had done.

"*Your love is killing me!*" Marco said loudly with mixed emotions. "What makes you say you love me? Maybe a couple of months from now you'll wake up, realize the severity of what happened, and hate me for this. Maybe right now you're blinded by love, and you don't see the gravity of the situation. If you were screaming and telling me that you hate me, it'd be a more natural and realistic reaction."

Sofia was standing and listening to Marco calmly. She felt Marco's frightful feelings of annoyance and disappointment. She was silent for a few seconds, and then she said, "So you want me to scream and yell at you and say that I hate you because of your honest mistake?" Sofia's voice was very stern and serious. "Because I know it wasn't intentional, and you just made a mistake… which is killing you! I trust you, and I believe in you." She paused before continuing, "As George Orwell said, 'Happiness can exist only in acceptance.' And I think with acceptance we can overcome any obstacles or challenges in life. *I accepted this with love!*" Sofia grabbed her tea and took a sip.

Marco was speechless.

"Marco, I just want to make something clear. If you're staying with me or want to continue this relationship just because you feel guilty, then I don't want it. I don't want you to stay with me out of obligation. We have to put this behind us in order to have a happy relationship in the future."

"You know that I'm not the kind of man who would stay in a relationship because of guilt. Please, never think about that and never bring it up again. Nothing that has occurred can ever change my feelings or desire to be with you. I want us to move forward and make more amazing memories."

Sofia started walking toward the living room, then turned and looked at Marco. "Come with me…"

Marco followed Sofia into the living room. She approached the piano and opened it up. "I want you to play for me…please. You need to practice; otherwise, you'll forget what I taught you."

Marco pulled Sofia to him, kissed her, looked into her eyes, and said, "My sweet little hummingbird…*your love is a gift, and I will treasure it forever!*"

Marco sat down at the piano and started playing *Moonlight Sonata*. Sofia sat on the couch next to the piano and quietly listened to him play.

Four Weeks Later—September 2017

SOFIA'S CAR—DAY

Sofia's cell phone rang; Marco was calling. Sofia picked it up.

"Hi."

"Sofia, how are you feeling? Did you get everything from the pharmacy?"

Sofia sounded tired. "I'm OK, but I didn't sleep well last night." She sighed. "This condition is so bothersome that all night long I was up and down taking showers, like a dozen times. I just left the pharmacy, and I got the antiviral medication for the outbreaks. This one is different because the other medication I had last month made me really sick and gave me terrible side effects. I'm hoping that this one will work better. There are only two main antiviral meds for this virus and nothing else."

"What about the prescription cream you told me about? Did you get that too? Maybe that will help you to minimize the itch."

"I didn't get it. First, I'll try this new medication and see if it helps. If so, then I don't need the cream."

"It can't hurt if you use both of them. Sofia, you have to try everything—this is about your health! You should go back and get the cream. Please do that."

"I'll do it next time, I promise."

Marco was getting a little agitated. "I don't understand you. What's wrong with you? You should be trying everything to feel better. Why don't you get it now? What's the big deal about getting a cream for your outbreaks?"

"OK, that prescription cream costs four hundred dollars, and my insurance doesn't cover it. So I'd have to pay for it out of pocket, and I can't spend four hundred dollars right now just for that tiny tube."

"You're crazy...because of that? I can pay for the cream. Why didn't you tell me? Please, go back and get the cream, and I'll give you the money when I see you."

"That's OK. There's no rush right now. I have the medication, and I can take that first, and then I'll get the cream."

"Sofia, I want you to go and get that cream, and I will give you the money later." Marco sounded serious and direct. "If you feel uncomfortable taking my money, perhaps you can make soup for me." He paused a little. "No...you always cook for me. You don't need to do that.

Then…hmm…you can buy me a gift instead, or this will be my gift to you. All right?"

After hearing all this from Marco, Sofia was stunned and confused. She felt very uncomfortable. "Marco, you don't need to give me money, but I will always make soup for you. Let's not talk about this anymore. I have to go now. My manager is calling me, and I'm late. Talk to you later."

Marco sensed that Sofia didn't like his comments, and he started laughing. "Sofia, I'm just joking! OK, go and I'll talk to you later. Sending my kisses…"

They both hung up the phone. Sofia looked confused and said to herself, "That was not a joke."

SOFIA'S APARTMENT—DAY

Sofia was lying down on the floor of her living room. She looked sick and was calling Jessie.

"Hi, honey. How are you?" Jessie was in her bedroom. She was in her wheelchair watching TV and resting her legs up on the bed.

"Not well." She sounded very weak. "I'm very dizzy and lying down on the floor. I was a little scared, so I wanted to talk to you."

"Oh, sweetheart…I'm so sorry. Did you eat?"

"I did. I took my medication half an hour ago after I ate, but it affects me so quickly. I can't function properly, and I can't even describe how I feel. I don't have any pain, but I'm nauseous and dizzy."

"Did you talk to your doctor and tell her that you get all these side effects? Maybe you shouldn't be taking these pills. I'm so angry about what you're going through."

"All the doctors are saying that these are the only medications for the herpes virus. So I've decided that if I have the outbreaks again next month, I'm not taking any medication. The only thing is that with the meds, the blisters heal much sooner. Without meds, they can last a couple of weeks. I don't know what to do…" She sighed. "When I take a dose, for the next three hours I can't focus or do anything. It makes me feel very weak, and the only thing that helps me a little bit is if I lie down flat. At least I don't get dizzy in this position."

"I don't know what to say, honey. You have to decide what to do with that medication. Hopefully, you won't have another outbreak next month. Let's pray for that."

"I'm hoping for that too!" Sofia paused a little bit. "Jessie, this morning I got all the goodies that you sent to Nick and me. I love the muffins and jams—you are *amazing*! Nick will be so happy to see his favorite cookies when he comes home from school."

"Oh, sweetheart, that's nothing. I wish I could do more. At least I can send you things. How's Marco? Is he helping you?"

"Oh, yes. He calls and texts me every day. You know he's very busy, works really hard, and can't see us often, but he usually comes over on the weekend."

"Oh, that's a huge help—calling and texting. What's wrong with him?" said Jessie angrily. "He should be coming more often and helping you with everything. He should be taking Nick to his basketball classes and show some responsibility to make things easier for you. You need his help. Look at you…how you're feeling. You can't drive anywhere in this condition. He should also be picking up your prescription meds from the pharmacy. By the way…did he give you money for the cream when he came to visit you over the weekend?"

"No, he forgot. But Jess, he always offers his help and always asks me if I need anything."

"And…what's your response?" Jessie tried to imitate Sofia's sweet voice, "'*No, thank you, I have everything I need.*' So he conveniently forgot to pay for the cream that you need because of his irresponsibility? This is bullshit! Sorry, honey, but I don't care anymore. He is so fucking wealthy…He's driving a half-million-dollar Ferrari, but he can't pay four hundred dollars for the cream? He is *soooo* cheap! Instead of coming once a week to your place, he should be there all the time, doing errands, grocery shopping, and even cooking. You always cook for him! Has he ever picked up dinner for you in the past four months while you were so sick and couldn't even get out of your place? *No!* Has he ever come with you to the hospital when you ended up in the ER and urgent care twenty-five times in the past four months? *No!* Only once has he taken you there, and that's a big deal? Has he ever asked you how much medical expense you've incurred in the past few months? *Of course not!* Does he understand how difficult it is for a single mom to raise a child under normal circumstances, let alone with unexpected medical bills? He doesn't care! Otherwise, he would have just done what needed to be done whether you asked him to or not!"

Jessie's voice was rising up. She was getting extremely furious. "You were unable to focus on your work or do anything for the past four months because of him. For God's sake, you had a catheter for an entire month, and you were still grocery shopping and cooking for him! Sofia, *what's wrong with you?* You need to love yourself first, take care of yourself, and think about yourself! Let him buy his own goddamn soup and dinner! You are making everything so easy for him…That's not right. Marco doesn't deserve a woman like you. He's in love with his money and himself and is afraid to spend a penny if it doesn't benefit him. Honey, you're the most gracious, beautiful, intelligent, and generous woman I know, and you deserve so much better—*so much better*! If I were you, I would've hired a lawyer and sued the shit out of him… That's what he deserves. What a selfish, greedy bastard!"

Sofia sighed. "Jessie, please stop! Marco is a good man, and I would never ever hurt or harm him. I don't want his money. The only thing I want from him is his love and for him to be more responsible and considerate." Sofia got very introspective. "Maybe I did something wrong. Maybe I should have asked him for things. Maybe that was my mistake, thinking that he would do it on his own. He knows me very well, and he knows what I love. When I'm not feeling well, sometimes I don't even know what I want." Sofia was in tears, and her voice began to shake. "For example, right now I don't want anything because I'm not feeling well, and if you asked me, 'Honey, would you like anything?' I'd say, "No, thank you,' because I don't know what I want! But when I got those muffins and jams this morning unexpectedly, I was so happy and really enjoyed them. Everything was delicious. But if he can't figure out on his own what a sick person might need, then I would never ask him. Why can't he figure it out on his own?"

"Because men are stupid…not all of them but most of them! That's why I have a dog! My Charlie is the best male I've ever had in my life."

Jessie looked at Charlie lying down next to her. After hearing Jessie's comment, Sofia started laughing and crying at the same time. Jessie cracked up too.

"Please, Sof…I'm sorry. I don't want to stress you out any more than you already are. I know how much you love this man, and he's very, very lucky. The only thing I wish right now is for you to get strong and healthy. You need to take care of yourself because Nick needs you more than anything. Now, I want you to close your eyes and just relax. Don't think about anything and try to meditate. I'll check on you later, OK?"

"OK…thanks, Jess. I love you and will talk to you later."

"Love you, too, honey."

MARCO'S OFFICE—DAY

Marco was sitting at his desk in his office, and someone was calling his cell phone. Marco picked up the phone. His father was calling.

"Hi, Marco."

"Hi, Dad. Happy early birthday! I know it's officially tomorrow, but since you'll be out of town tomorrow, I thought we could get together tonight, and then you can have two days of birthday celebration."

Carlos chuckled. "Although I'll be out of town, you could still call me tomorrow…I do have my cell phone! Thanks anyways! Tonight sounds good. What time are you planning to pick me up?"

"Sofia and I will be at your place at seven thirty. We'll have fun tonight. OK, Dad, take it easy and see you soon."

"OK, then. See you later, son."

ROYAL RUAL HOTEL—EVENING

The SUV was parked in front of the Royal Rual Hotel, and the valets were helping Sofia, Marco, and Carlos get out of the car. Once everyone was out, they entered the hotel.

Marco, Sofia, and Carlos were seated at a table in the restaurant, reviewing the menus. Carlos looked very cheerful about the fact that he was celebrating his birthday with Sofia and Marco. A waiter approached their table to take their order. Meanwhile, in the corner of the restaurant, there was a live band that was playing dinner music.

"Good evening! Are you ready to order your drinks?" a young waiter asked.

"Yes. Can we have three glasses of Moet & Chandon Brut Imperial Rosé?" Marco responded.

"Absolutely, sir. Anything else right now?"

"We still need some time for our orders," Marco answered respectfully.

"Of course. Take your time—no rush," the waiter said, and he left the table. Sofia got the gift that she'd bought for Marco's dad and handed it to Carlos.

"Carlos, happy birthday! This is nothing big, but it's from my heart. I hope you like it."

"Thank you, dear. You don't need to give me anything, but the best gift is when it comes from the heart. That's what matters. I'm not going to open it now because today isn't officially my birthday, and they say it's bad luck if you open your gifts before your birthday! So I'll open it tomorrow. But thanks again for thinking of me, and most importantly, I'm grateful that you're here with me and my son." Carlos really liked Sofia, and he was truly happy that she was there with him and Marco.

"Of course, you can open it anytime. I'm happy to be here with you to celebrate your birthday," Sofia said lovingly.

Marco leaned over and kissed Sofia. He was so joyful and content that she was there with him. The waiter brought their drinks and placed them on the table. Everyone picked up their glasses, and in unison, they all said, "Cheers," to each other and sipped their champagne.

Then, while listening to the music, Carlos got up and said, "I'm going to dance."

He saw two ladies sitting quietly at the next table, and he asked one of them to dance with him. One of the ladies got up and followed Carlos to the dance floor, and they started dancing. Sofia and Marco were watching them and smiling. Then Marco grabbed Sofia, and they both headed to the dance floor. Once they got to the floor, the music ended, but in a few seconds, the singer started a new song: "I Just Called to Say I Love You" by Stevie Wonder. Sofia and Marco were so happy to hear that song because it was one of their favorites. They started dancing together, embracing each other and kissing. While dancing Marco sang along:

> *I just called to say I love you*
> *I just called to say how much I care*
> *I just called to say I love you*

"I love you, Sofia," he said.

This was the first time Marco ever told Sofia that he loved her. Sofia's eyes got big, and she was so thrilled to hear that from Marco. "Really? You love me..." Sofia said warmly and lovingly.

Marco shifted quickly and said, "I love you, but don't be excited. I'm not there yet, but I'm getting there."

Sofia's face totally changed, but she didn't want to show her disappointment, so she continued dancing. She didn't want to spoil Marco's father's birthday, so she kept smiling and dancing even though she was hurt. Marco's father looked very excited and animated while he was dancing with his new lady friend.

MARCO'S CAR—MIDNIGHT

After the birthday dinner, Marco dropped Sofia off at her apartment. He had just parked the car and was getting ready to get out of the car to escort Sofia to her front door. She stopped him.

"Marco, I have to say this to you because I keep thinking about it. Tonight, when we were dancing, you said, 'I love you, Sofia, but don't be excited. I'm not there yet, but I'm getting there.' I didn't want to spoil your father's birthday because he was so happy and was enjoying his evening fully, so I respected his celebration. But I really don't understand your comment about me not getting excited. It made me feel like I need to work harder to deserve your love! What was that all about? That comment was very upsetting and hurtful. If you're not sure about your feelings, about whether you love me, then don't say anything until you are! Nobody asked you to say it. I was so thrilled to hear it from you at that perfect moment while we were dancing, but you spoiled it completely." Sofia was heartbroken. "Even if you say it now, a million times, it won't have the same meaning. I felt so touched and moved when you were singing and you said, '*I love you, Sofia.*' But you truly ruined that special moment for me…and I've waited a long time to hear you say that."

"I am *so* sorry…I'm really very sorry. You're right! It wasn't the right thing to say, but I shocked myself when I said, 'I love you.' It happened so unexpectedly, and I wasn't ready." Marco sounded embarrassed and didn't know what to say.

"You weren't ready for what?" Sofia asked.

"I don't know. When I said that, I was surprised. It happened so automatically and quickly…" He sighed. "I apologize. I shouldn't have said that."

"When I say, 'I love you,' it comes from my heart and soul so naturally and easily. I don't need to think about it…I just feel it. Every cell of my body feels the love I have for you. Throughout our relationship I tried to show you my love with the simple things that I did. For me, those simple gestures show true care and love. I don't know how to express my love any other way. But that comment tonight was very, very hurtful. Please don't hurt me with comments like that again." Sofia paused. "I have to go now—I'm very tired."

Sofia opened the door and got out of the car. Marco also got out and walked towards Sofia. He grabbed her hand and walked with her to her apartment. They both stood in front of the apartment door. Sofia looked tired, but Marco hugged and kissed her.

"I'm so happy that you came to celebrate my father's birthday."

"He really had a good time," Sofia replied. Before she opened her apartment door, she softly said, "Love you!"

"I love you, too…but I'm not in love with you," Marco responded.

After Marco said that, Sofia looked at him, paused, and then faintly smiled. "Good night, Marco."

Sofia opened her apartment door and entered her place.

SOFIA'S APARTMENT, BEDROOM—NEXT MORNING

Sofia was in her bed, still sleeping, when Nick ran into the bedroom. "Mom…Mom…wake up! It's seven thirty. I'll be late for school!"

Sofia could not even open her eyes. She looked very sick and sounded depressed. "Nick, you need to walk to school today. I can't get up—I'm sorry. I'm sick. Don't forget your lunch money." Sofia was wrecked.

Nick had never seen his mom like this. He looked very concerned and was a little bit scared. "Mom, are you OK? Do you need anything?"

"No…I'm OK! Just go. Go or you'll be late." Sofia insisted that Nick leave. Nick left the room, but he looked very concerned. Sofia was in her bed covered by her blanket, and her eyes were closed. She heard the apartment door close. Nick was gone. Sofia slowly opened her eyes and started moving in her bed. She picked up her phone and checked to see if anyone had called or texted her. She got up from her bed and felt that she must look awful. She went straight to the bathroom, looked in the mirror, and saw that her eyes were red and swollen. Then she washed her face. She came out from the bathroom still wearing her pj's and walked to the kitchen. She put the electric kettle on to boil some water for her tea. She took a teacup out of the cabinet and put a tea bag inside the cup. She went to the dining room and picked up her laptop. Then she went back to the kitchen, sat down at the table, and opened her laptop. She started writing a letter to Marco.

> Dear Marco,
>
> I am writing this letter with much love. After our conversation yesterday, I had a wake-up call, and I was awake all night thinking about our relationship. The one thing that I finally understand is that I'm with a man who loves and cares about me as a friend but who is truly not in love with me. If these past eight months are any indication of your true feelings for me, then you'll never fall in love with me. I remember so clearly on our third date that you told me the following: "I don't believe it when people say it takes time to fall in love with a person, like after five or six months you've had enough time, and by then you should be in love with your partner. It doesn't work like that for me. Either I fall in love with a woman right in the beginning or I never do."

These are your true words! I don't want or need that kind of relationship. It's not healthy or fair for either of us—and especially not for my son. I'm a responsible mother raising a teenager, and I can't deal with a casual relationship. This is definitely not what I want. I know that the last four months have been extremely emotional for both of us, and I think now it's time for me to think rationally and focus on healing myself. One thing I want you to know is that my feelings for you have always been very strong and genuine, and I want you to find the same thing with someone that you can fall in love with. I'm very thankful and appreciative for the memories that we created together and especially grateful for finally knowing how to accept, value, and love myself first and foremost. As Rumi said in one of his poems, "He said, 'How do you benefit from this life?' / I said, 'By keeping true to myself.'" So I want to be true to myself just as I want to have peace, bliss, and harmony. And I want the same for you. It's been extremely difficult for me to write this farewell letter, but I know this is the right thing to do in order for both of us to move on. I hope you'll find love and happiness in the future.

>Love,
>Sofia

Sofia took a deep breath, then clicked the send button on the email and closed her laptop.

Two and a Half Months Later

PUBLIC PARK—MORNING

Sofia was jogging when her phone rang. She looked at her phone and saw that Maddie was calling her. She stopped jogging and answered it.

"Hi, Maddie!"

"My Sofia…how are you? I think of you every day."

"Oh, Maddie, I love you! I'm doing better, and I feel great this morning. I'm in the park enjoying this beautiful day." Sofia was breathing fast. "I was just jogging."

Maddie was driving. "I have to say this because I've been thinking about it. I know it hasn't been even three months since you broke up with Marco, and that's not very long. It's been a very, very difficult time for you, especially with everything you went through this past summer. It's really easy for me to simply say, 'Sofia, please forget about him and move on,' but I know it's not going to be easy for you. The way he behaved and treated you after all the love you gave to him convinces me that he didn't deserve a woman like you. For me, he is a *coward*! At least he should have responded to your email, or he should have said something. I can't believe he just walked away like that. But I want you to know that I'm here for you. I love you, and I'm very sure that this universe is preparing something very special for you because you're a woman that deserves everything beautiful. The love that you gave to this man was so pure and precious that there's no way that God won't reward you with the same gift. What you gave to him will come back to you because you're worth it and you absolutely deserve it."

Sofia was quiet, and while hearing all these touching words from Maddie, she got teary. "I'm so lucky that you're my dear friend. Thank you for being there for me and helping me through this."

"Oh, Sofia! Of course I'm here for you, and I know that everything will be just fine. You are very strong, and soon you'll be flying again like a happy hummingbird. Now I'm calling you a hummingbird!"

Maddie chuckled. Sofia chuckled, too, and her mood changed a little bit. She wiped her tears away.

"Oh, by the way, you reminded me of a dream that I had last night."

"Really? What was it?"

Sofia started describing her dream in detail. "It was a very strange dream, actually. I dreamed that my curly hair was like the nest of a little hummingbird. I put my hand into my hair and found this tiny hummingbird. I was holding it in my palm, and it was looking at me. I knew that it was hungry, but I didn't have anything at home except strawberry yogurt, so I decided to give it some." Sofia chuckled. "And it started eating the yogurt! Then it flew back into my hair. That was really weird… My hair was a hummingbird's nest." Sofia paused and suddenly she had a thought. "Maddie, I've gotta go—I'll call you later."

Sofia started jogging back to her car. When she reached it, she got in and drove home quickly, her mind racing with a million thoughts. She opened the door to her apartment, ran to her room, sat down with her computer, and started typing her story:

A Hummingbird's Nest.

About the Author

Growing up in the country of Georgia, Russo began her passion for writing by expressing her thoughts, dreams, and goals in her simple childhood diary, which she retains to this day. By writing stories and poetry, she became an adventurer, taking on different personas and experiencing the heartache and happiness of the human spirit through the written word. Russo earned a BA in Mass Media Studies and Television Broadcasting at the University of Westminster in London and that catapulted her into international television broadcasting and production. But her dreams only began being truly fulfilled after she moved to the US and published her poetry collection, titled *A Hummingbird's Reminder*, and her debut novel, *A Hummingbird's Nest*.

Also by Russo Shanidze

www.ingramcontent.com/pod-product-compliance
Lightning Source LLC
LaVergne TN
LVHW011832060526
838200LV00053B/3977